Contents

CHAPTER: 1. SONY RETURNS

"When the World is at Peace, a gentleman keeps his Sword by his side."
- Sun Tsu, author of the Art of War

As Sony walks down the descending steps of the plane that just pulled up at Gatwick airport, he feels a strange sense of nosier; as though he is a stranger coming home. Each step holds a paramount significance; years of training and international fighting have now made him return to where it all started. His gaze cuts through the concrete surroundings, past the hordes of crowds, shops, cars and trucks manoeuvring and behind them he sees the destination clearly in his mind: CRYSTAL PALACE SPORTS CENTRE in South London (the halls of greatness for martial artists of his day) and the challenges that await him. However, despite the gravity of the moment, there is a heavier thought that comes to mind; bearing this thought he passes through the inspection, takes his bag and then heads for the train. His journey feels tedious, but the length of his travels are broken by passing thoughts of his journeys as a youth to Brighton beach with his friends Roger and William; trying to pull girls in the summer (naturally gravitating towards the ones with the tightest swimsuits). These pleasant glimpses in time were occasionally broken by the stares and sense of uneasiness coming from other passengers towards him, he laughs in his head "well some things will never change, England, the only country in the world where every one's angry for no reason". In truth he was used to it: when one reaches such a formidable level of fighting, the confidence and power emanating from the individual is always noticeable by the average person. The narrowness of the train with its blue cotton seating all screamed British to him.

Now at Brompton cemetery; unwavering in its Italian design inherited from the previous century. He walks through the nature inspired designs of the gardens, the carefully trimmed grass and patches of planted flowers (reflecting the peace he hopes his own heart will carry in this movement). He halts in front of a wooden chair carved from the wood of a bonsai tree; the wood is dark, but smooth and the waves that run across it are a throne giving honour to its patron, and his name is bellow it inscribed on a rectangular gold plate: Edward Williams, 1920. Sony kneels with his left knee and then with his right. He bows on the grass to pay his respects to the man who inspired his martial art training: his great grandfather.

Once a fair minded sailor working for the East India Company, Edward Williams travelled across the Far East until he had a certain experience in Japan that changed his life. He was an aggressive man and a brawler, having come from an extremely 'passionate' and poor Irish family with a non-compromising view of the evil of Protestants. He was raised with no hopes or ambitions and at the age of twelve he aspired to become a carpenter. One day he was approached by a young sailor who wanted a small box built for his travels. This event marked the change in the Irishman's life that would lead to him sailing the oceans. A year later they were assigned the duty of carrying a payment of gold to the Emperor of Japan. Off course the lowly sailors were not permitted to take part in the venture when on land and were paid duly then sent to explore the city; returning to set sail the following morning. Whilst the lads were walking through the streets of Tokyo (searching for prostitutes, pubs and food) a sweet smell like that of a lotus flower hit Edward's nose; compelling him to turn his head. So his eyes caught a Japanese woman sitting on the ground pouring tea and there was an instant bulge in his pants as he scanned the woman up and down; her blue kimino and tied hair added to an exotic beauty in Edward's eyes. He sat next to her and began to talk, "ay, yur a pretty little girly aint ya? How bout we jump in the sack somewhere?" The woman was silent (unwavering in her concentration of the tea pouring). He persisted and dropped a few coins in front her. This time she glared at him and her eyes were still and cold with complete focus. Edward felt a shock run through his spine and a sharp pain in his stomach which made crippling fear attach to him. "What the hell was that, who the hell are ya!!" Turning to run he slams into the legs of a Samurai standing in front of him, majestic in image with his sword's scabbard on his hip. He loosely smiles at Edward and grabs him by his shoulder; hoisting him to his feet. To his left is a short, white man in a well fitted grey suit. The Samurai begins to speak and the translator conveys the meaning: "you fool! You seek trouble with someone far beyond your mental abilities. You are a hostile man, yet a great fighter, but your mind is weak and for the sake of your future generations you must perfect yourself". Edward's paralysis had now gone and was overshadowed by the smoke of confusion angering him. "What the hell are you talking about boy, who the hell are you!!" The man's face moved from the smile to a disgusting snarl; "I am a captain of his majesty's army. My sword is sharper than your mind and you would have never approached this woman if you knew the essence of the tea ceremony". With that remark the Samurai captain left Edward in confusion. The woman rose to her feet and gave Edward the tea she had prepared. She then jumped into a carriage and disappeared. This became a pivoting point in Edward's life; the experience was fast moving, yet clear in message and the characteristics of his superstitious upbringing compelled him to accept the message.

He used the rest of his wages to buy tea and sailed back to England the next day. Leaving the East India Company he became a tea merchant settling at Coombe Cliff Gardens (the place for traders of the time); hoping to one day discover the secret of his experience. On a winters day when he was trading a Japanese man approached him. "I hear you sell Japanese tea here?" As Edward looked up at the man he sure the handle of a Samurai sword poking from his trousers. "Indeed we do", Edward said whilst passing the tea to him. As the man began to go into his pocket to pay Edward held his hand up, "no, don't worry about it mate. What is it that you do?" "I run a martial arts dojo in the city, why?" "Well I think that's how we can square up: you show me what you do and whenever you're around you can count on me for green tea. I think that's a bargain personally", Edward riddled with a grin. The customer was amused, "indeed it is, you have a deal". The men then exchanged address for tea. At this point in time Sony's grandfather: David, was about eight years old. He and his father attended the demonstration at the Bermondsey gym where the master performed a sword kata (sequence). His movements were so elegant and graceful, yet you could hear the sword slicing the air; they could feel the dangerous intent of each movement. Edward looked at the master's eyes and sure the same look as the woman pouring tea all those years ago in Japan. He then looked at his son and sure the unwavering astonishment and concentration on the child's face. After the demonstration Edward approached the master and relayed the story of his life to him. "I'm too old to learn this stuff now, but teach my son; he can understand what I was never able to in my lifetime".

And so began the legacy of the William family's martial arts and now Sony (the fourth generation to inherit the arts) pays homage to his ancestor; he is seeking guidance, he feels lost. Through his father, Sony had been practicing Jujitsu from the age of five (taught that he must discover the secret of his family's martial arts). At the age of fifteen he became discontented with the softness of jujitsu and felt the style was not giving him the power that he wanted. As such, he went on a search for the most powerful style of martial arts. After three years of tedious research he finally joined a school in Shirley practicing Kyokushinkai Karate. From his first lesson he was confident that this was the style for him; the overt violence and tough training in the sparring, the practical steps behind kata and the focus on conditioning the body ticked all the boxes for the young warrior. He practiced this style for the next five years and went on to compete in hundreds of tournaments internationally; even taking part in the famous one hundred man knockdown tournament. However (through all the fighting and travelling) he still feels unfulfilled and his recent training has been clouded by an eerie feeling; as though this tournament was different. At this desperate moment, he is praying that his forefather will guide him. Afterwards, taking a deep breath, Sony hoists himself to his feet, making his way out.

Exiting (although he is faced with exactly the same dilemma as when he walked in) he puts that aside and began to get excited and uplifted; his thoughts were now at the dancing festival he was on his way to. Finally, after a year of hard training he would get to see his old friends; share a drink, some food, stories and lastly to spend some time with the love that he left behind in London: Linda. The moment has arrived and Sony stands outside the majestic figure of Crystal Palace national sports centre (underneath and surrounding it is the athletics track equipped with thousands of stadium seats). Even now, at eight o' clock there are runners burning the rubber on the red track; complying diligently with white lines partitioning it (the young athletes pouring sweat so intense that even Sony who stands on the bridge that separates the two structures can feel the intensity of their work out). He takes a deep breath and walking towards the towering building and entering he passes the reception desk and walks towards the sports hall; he can hear the laughing and loud booms of the eighty's sounds. Walking through the room patterned by spinning circles of light coming from the large, silver disco ball on the ceiling gave the party feel intended. The sounds of disco had split groups of women bouncing choreographed dancing sequences. Around them (naturally) were men trying to lure them into a pair of. There were groups of people shout talking added to lose of drinks stinking the place out with vodka and beer scents. Hutched in the corner with a bottle of Guinness in his hand (almost as dark as himself) and long, thick dreadlocks that rocked as he nodded his head was Roger. Sony's heart started to race with even more excitement (partly spurred on by how bulky Roger had become: he had obviously been training hard; he guessed his sleeveless black top and cut jeans where his tools for showing of). "Just like him" Sony thought. They were only twelve when they first met, but even then they knew they would be friends for a long time; they were so similar.

Roger: descended from a family of black Liverpudlians his family had lived in South Norwood for four generations. However it was by no means easy; there was still a considerable degree of racism through the decades his family had lived there, their entire survival depended on their resilience. It is of then no surprise that from the age of ten he began training in the legendary Mckenzie boxer's pub in Thornton Heath. He excelled and at the age of fifteen began entering underground school competitions (of which he was undefeated in twenty matches); it was on his twentieth fight that he and Sony became acquainted. Young Sony walked into the concrete setting, excited and thrilled. He bought a pint and sat at the front. There was no cage, no lines, only the encircled crowd of teenagers as the ring. The 'referee' stood between the two young men; he was a skinny lad that would not intimidate anyone in the slightest if it wasn't for the scars all across his body as he paraded bare chested. He turned to the fighters, "listen boys, no shots below the waist, no rounds and no pussying out. I want a nice, bloody fight". He blew a whistle and the opponents started throwing punches at each other. They exchanged blow for blow and although the other boy was big and chubby this made no difference to the impact of Roger's punches. The two were slamming blows all over each other with uppercuts, swings and jabs but neither one would give in and by the first three minutes they were already bleeding heavily. Sony sat there in admiration of the violence and strength, but all the while he was calculating how his Jujitsu would work against it (sure the strength the two had was impressive but there was no strategy; against a real fighter they would surely meet their end). But then in the fourth minute Roger changed tactics: he began evading the other boy's jabs, that is, until the punch that he was waiting for arrived; the boy swung for Roger this time from his left arm, Roger lunged to the side of the attack and hit the boy's shoulder to the travelling direction of the punch, making him fall under the additional gravity and into Roger's awesome uppercut in his chin (achieving a KO). Sony was astonished; he underestimated his peer. The crowd howled and screamed their love for the bloody victory. Sony went to the shoddy, broken down table were the beers were served. He suddenly feels a sharp pinch in his buttocks and turned around to see a tall girl (dressed basically in nothing) smiling at him. "Buy me a drink hot stuff" Sony was stunned with embarrassment; he hadn't had much experience with girls and he just stood their goggling at her. "Who the fuck is this!!" Sony turned around to see Roger standing there (with cuts across his face) breathing heavily and fast, his eyes sharp with anger. Before Sony could even explain himself Roger sent a punch which didn't even take form from Sony's viewpoint as he was already turning his back, grabbing the arm over his shoulder, bending his knees and then throwing Roger past him. He shot through the air like an arrow; ten metres away. Roger opened his eyes and looked up to the ceiling and dangling in mid-air was a Guinness with Sony's hand wrapped around it. He helped Roger to his feet and that was the day the two joined forces on the quest for the most proficient fighting style.

And there he was after so many years, the two had been training to be the most powerful fighters. Sony walked towards him and Roger's eyes glanced to his direction; a swav smile formed on his face. At the same time that he was walking the corner of his eye caught a slightly chubby gentleman wearing a light blue suit and a t shirt underneath (reflecting as much the slick youthfulness of his character as his gelled hair did): it was Luke. Luke walked towards Roger and began whispering; no doubt about the good time he was going to have when he got home. Roger pointed towards Sony and the chubby man's eyes caught Sony and lit up. There was then a large, toothy smile that formed around his face. As Sony stepped in the presence of the two men he was a well fitted piece in a puzzle. Luke hugged Sony, shouting "the man of the hour is here! We're glad to see you mate", the two men then clasped hands.

Luke Brentford; a descendant of the infamous Carew family and inheritor to a small fortune as a consequence of his mother inheriting a reasonable sum from the sale of her ancestor's Norbury manor farm house to the council. His family were well known in Croydon and loved by old timers as the rhetoric of a long lost London. His mother invested the money into his first business as a town developer at the age of seventeen. The middle class spirit of his family in Pollards Hill rubbed off on him from a young age and he pursued his indoctrinated viewpoint of being better than everyone else. This was not only applied business wise but also physically and as a result he had a strong desire to become the best fighter in the UK. In seeking the fighting discipline that would give him the best start, he found a home in a small Kyokushinkai karate school in Shirley based in a church hall (he quickly developed in the robust style and by the age of seventeen he was already a blue belt). One hot summer's day, the students were in a park close to the dojo sparring; the slams of kicks and the rickashay of blocks could be heard throughout the perimeters. Luke was sitting on the well cut grass drinking a bottle of water when past the stretch of bushes behind him leading to a station of trees he heard loud noises (the type that only one from the world of fighters would recognise). Hearing this he decides to walk towards the sound, eventually reaching a patch of dry mud covered by three trees providing a cool shade with some shafts of light. In the centre of this serene setting were Sony and Roger training intensely. The obvious boxing conventions of Roger's hooks and locks of Sony's jujitsu struck a chord in Luke's heart: so devoted had he become to this Kyokushin style that the thought of separate styles being practiced was in his eyes, unforgiveable. "Oi that looks really crap; what are you guys doing?" He spouted. "Mind your own business!" Responded Roger (his temper evident in the vein pumping on his temple). Sony stayed quite; engrossed in the training session just passed, thinking deeply into his flaws and how to eradicate them. Luke started to stare down Roger and folded his arms. There was now complete silence and Roger refused to back down: he strode towards Luke proudly, chest pumped out, to receive a thorough kick in his stomach; leaving him gasping for air on the ground. Sony snapped out of his daydream and ran towards Luke (with no contemplation of what exactly brought Roger to his knees) who simply swung a fist, but Sony dodged and grabbed him to execute a throw, only to find a knee that lifted him off his feet and then an elbow to his shoulder; leaving his arm in a paralysed state (which became evident from the high pitch screech he emitted). There was then a storm of kyokushinkai students looking panic stricken and naturally prepared for engagement. Sensei David Leming (a powerful and majestic figure) marched in front of the students; his gi(uniform) appeared to radiate in shafts of light. "Well then, what happened here?" Luke became instantly humbled by the adult and with a tilted head he said "we were just training sensei. I don't know my own strength, I guess". Sony and Roger looked up at the man talking; his deep voice, jet black hair and streamed eyesight (along with the dizziness experienced by the confrontation) made the figure look like a Demi god. The two boys rose to their feet and stood in front of the master (embarrassed by the defeat they had just experienced). "So what do you guys practice?" "Jujitsu and boxing but we're looking for a club" Sony said hastily; halting Roger from denying them an opportunity out of pride. "Well then, come to the club (I'm sure you'll enjoy it) but only come if you're serious; our style is not for the light hearted". From then on the three boys trained together. Luke was assigned the duty of 'showing them the ropes' and as he got to know them he warmed to them and vice versa; not least because of the competitive edge they all had.

So many years ago and so many changes. They now stood as men; proficient in their own rights as formidable warriors. But today, none of that was at the forefronts of their minds. Today they were not rivals, today they were brothers. They drank together, laughed and spoke of their independent adventures; from women, to money and martial arts. "Oi, talking of lasses, there's your heart stopper", Roger remarked; pointing toward a crowd of females. There they were, (bouncing up and down to the chants of psychedelic sounds) the three diamonds at the party; their beauty outshone the competition by miles. Luke's love: madam Louise (in conventional stylish jeans and a white top), Roger's Kate (in a short skirt and tank top) and finally dressed in a long, white daachikee with a big ink heart sewed on as well as a light brown facial complexion (that was in no contrast to her long, flowing hair that waved in excitement): Linda. Sony's eyes began to narrow and he fell into his own trance of passion and yes; it was just that moment: the Rumba moment. Sony didn't hold back: (the moment grabbed him) he slowly walked up to Linda robotically and took her hand. When she sure him she didn't speak; instead they twirled with each other and every time she spun closer to him her hips moved slowly and sensationally; her breath and chest registered with Sony's senses (and as a result his crutch as well).

When the dance finished she fell into his arms and dragged him out of the leisure centre and through the darkness of the park where she leaned him against a tree and kissed him. The moment was so intense that still no words were spoken (but they both knew the dialogue); she thought "I thought you were never going to come back" and his thoughts were "I would never forget you. I love you so such". And with that he returned to her flat in Anerley and they embraced each other.

CHAPTER 2: MORNING TIME

Sony woke up the next morning the happiest he's ever been; underneath the dark purple sheets with the love of his life. The curtains were drawn and the room was shaded by the dark red reflection of the wallpapers. They were both still sweating from the night before and he could feel her soft breathing against the hairs on his chest. He looked at her and took a deep breath (taking the moment into his lungs); the joy of true companionship. Linda's ears twitched at the sound and her long, flowing hair began to brush softly up his body as she awoke; her torso rose and she looked at him with a dizzied expression and pushing her chest against his, she kissed him. "Morning you" she said with a warm smile on her face (as though he had never been away). She glances at her windowsill, rolled smoothly out of the bed and pulled the curtains sharply; allowing the sunlight to bolt through the windows and hit the bed as though it was asking Sony to come and meet the day. On the windowsill a silver grinder stood before a cigarette, a packet of Rizals and a packet of light green marijuana. She begins grinding the marijuana and turns to face Sony, "so, what should we do today then?" Sony looks at her with a cockily raised eyebrow, "you tell me: you're the Londoner. All I wanna know is what we're having for breakfast; I hope it's not that stuff". Linda giggled and sighed deeply, "well that's weird: a tourist born in London. I may have to fleece you: fifty quid for your complementary fruit salad". There was no response from Sony; instead his eyebrow sank and he crooked his head to the side as a gesture of sarcasm, by this time the spliff was now rolled; she lit it and then inhaled.

Meanwhile, in the suburbs of Purley Way and at the highest floors of the Hilton hotel in a VIP suite kitted with a ceramic Jacuzzi, a king sized bed and an en suite bathroom (the size of someone like Linda's living room) Luke and madam Louise lay on the floor next to a vintage bottle of champagne beside a packet of open condoms (he in his boxers and vest and she in her nickers and bra) lying with her leg stretched over his waist. She just about managed to open her eyes and the feeling of her alcohol laden stomach at first prevented her from moving, until she consciously yanked her back upwards and gave Luke a condescending light slap across his face. "Come on you, wake up, order breakfast". She stood up whilst Luke was left to wake from his hung over slumber. His memory returned to him eventually and he became grounded in his environment (then consciousness turned to annoyance) as he stood up and flattened himself on the bed. By this time Louise was already in the Jacuzzi with her bra removed and a smug look on her face. "What the hell is your problem woman? If you want food, go and call room service yourself. I don't even know how or why I've spent money on all this stuff". Her smug grin remained and she rolled back her shoulders, stretching out her arms, pushing her breasts forward. "I think we both know why: I have requirements from my men and one way or another I get what I want". Luke stared blankly at her (feeling that taking orders was about to compromise his manhood) but still he felt compelled to pick up the phone. "She's so spoilt" he thought and then he began to dial.

"The life of a working man" thought Roger as he starred at the punching bag (or the self-improvised punching bag); a sack of sand with a thick cord of rope wrapped tightly around it, attached to a nail on the ceiling suspending it. It was six o' clock in the morning and he and his girlfriend had made love until sunrise, after that he couldn't sleep which was not unusual for him: he had so much energy that on occasion it kept his body up (even though his mind was worn out). Looking at the white duvet on the floor with no mattress (only pillows) and sleeping peacefully on her side was Kate; worn out from her night shift at the bar she worked at in Coulsdon. As he focused intently on her arm he sure the wail marks of the burns given to her by those bastard drug dealers of whom she called cousins. The anger pained his heart, left his stomach aching and the tears manifested themselves as kicks and punches; each one breaking the illusion that he could do something about it. "It was a sin" he thought: "to harm a creature so wonderful". Her bright yellow hair gave testimony in his eyes and he slammed his foot into the bag so hard that the rope snapped of the nail and crashed on the ground. She woke up; unaware of the reasons behind this and instead glanced at Roger with pride. "Wow! I wish I was awake to see that" she said in her high pitched accent. "Needed to blow of some steam before I going to work" he shrugged and he began to boil the kettle on top of the old, unclean washing machine in his studio flat. She jumped to her feet and (wearing his t shirt and shorts) went into the fridge; taking out eggs, bread and bacon. "What are you doing?" He enquired. "Making breakfast off course" she answered. "Go back to bed and sleep". She walked over to him and began to rub his arm, "if you think I'm goanna let those big arms leave with no fuel, you must be having a laugh". The truth was that Roger didn't feel like eating, but he knew that she cared and even though his job as a Whitgift shopping centre security guard didn't require the energy that her stodgy breakfast would give him. He sat down and ate with her. After which he put on his uniform to shoot of to his uninspiring, bill paying job.

CHAPTER 3: LINDA'S FREEDOM

'Let the swordsman disregard from the first what may come out of the engagement, let him keep his mind clear of such thoughts. For the first principle of swordsmanship is a thorough insight into heavenly reason, which works out according to the chance circumstances; the rest is of no concern to the swordsman himself.'
  -Ichiun Odagiri: 2nd grandmaster of
  Mujuushin Kenjutsu Samurai sword school

The water was clear and glided smoothly; it circled the small island on a bed of pebbles, imbecilic of the park at Phipps Bridge in Mitcham. There were planted beds of white, red and purple roses poised proudly in their prime magnificence; creatively placed on circular, rectangular and crescent shaped beds (giving testimony to the legacy of British landscaping). And in the centre of it (as though it was the park's axis) a tall perfectly straight tree with twisted arms and light green fingers provided the shade under which Linda and Sony sat, feeding each other tropical fruit (melon, mango etc.); fruits that Linda was all too familiar with being the daughter of an Indian mother. Her light brown skin was radiant from the sunlight and her nose sharp, her hips slender yet filled and her eyes curled perfectly. Sony was truly in awe of her as he pondered his luck: he aspired to be a legend and she was one. She began to role another joint and her white, flower power t shirt and long skirt hit home to Sony as a contrast to the first day he met her. "So what have you been up to whilst I've been gone?" Said Sony, "same old, babes: nothing's changed". Her answer didn't surprise him in the least; she always went with the flow, so free and careless, not a worry in the world. As she blew the smoke it swayed in the light breeze that broke humidity; waving like a dancer; like it was a part of her. Like it was a hologram of when she was fourteen at the Paula Lennine School of dance in Addiscombe (bouncing freely to the ballet movements she was being taught). The smoke hit Sony's face just like the young girl's foot had kicked him all those years ago when they first met. "What a strange twist of face" he was thinking; casting a glimpsing thought to the day his dad brought him to the school to see the teacher: an 'old friend' (the same 'old friend' that he used to disappear with) leaving Sony at the dance school to watch the practice. Linda stretched her legs in the park with toned calves (the same toned calves that had driven him to her all those years ago). "So what state's the country in?" "Same as always: screwing up due to the whims of these political cunts". Sony smiled to himself; he was wanting to start a sharp debate (one of the many things he missed about her). "Arrrrre! Come on, they're not all that bad", "don't be an idiot! Where should we start; the fact that they obviously don't care about the poor, the wars they start or the crooked ways they run our society", "well I suppose you drug loving hippies have the answer", "screw you! Weed isn't a drug and hippies love, we don't fight. If we ran the world, everything would be different!" "Nah, don't think so babe (even you're not that smart) I mean, what would be your economic policy: legalise narcotics. Or..." "Wait right there. I have an English degree and graduated with honours. What do you have? A couple of black belts!" Sony looked at her and chuckled; falling back on the grass on his belly. "So easy!" He spouted and she pounced on his back, "I heard that. You're such a fool". He just sat there in silence; using the conversation as ammunition for a daydream about her:

In October 1968 at Grosvenor square; protesting with her friend Tariq Ali: the leader of the anti-Vietnam demonstration. He could see her debating the issues and rallying students to the cause (she was of course one of the protest's architects). She stared at Sony's hands; rubber coated from the tireless Kyokushinkai training on trees, hot sand and everywhere he could break the nerve endings (they felt like biker gloves). "Have you found what you were looking for yet?" "Not yet" Sony sighs (reluctant to expand). "Sometimes the things we look for find us instead yuno", "guess so" replied Sony (trying to break the dialogue of the topic). "Ah! I have a surprise for you!" She leaped to her feet; reaching for her bag with an odd grin on her face (like she was cunningly hiding something); her stretched smile exposing her slightly discoloured teeth was a sure sign of this to Sony. Both of her hands were inside the bag and she began to lift, hoisting her surprise. Sony began to see a pile of utensils emerge from the bag: at first a tea whisk, two small bowls and a ladle seated on a small metal pot, which in turn was seated on a slightly larger red pot. Sony was bemused but excited so he held his inquisitiveness in and focused on what she was doing. She continued to rummage through her bag and pulled out some wood chips, tissue and at last a small container with tea bags inside of it. At last Sony asked the question: "What's this then?" Linda smiled cheekily, "well, whilst you were away I met a guy through a friend at a karaoke bar and I asked him what Japanese stuff I could do to surprise my boyfriend (I told him you did karate) and he showed me this thing; it's called the way of tea he said (all the best fighters in Japan do it before tournaments)." "Is it? I've never met a fighter who spoke about that. How can tea help you to fight? Sounds like bullshit to me" Sony responded proudly. He hated being told new things about martial arts from people who weren't masters and the fact that this came from his girlfriend added insult to injury. Linda was now annoyed (which was rare) and her eyes were always a clear sign of this. Sony recognised this and began to simmer down. "I was trying to do something nice for you!" Ungrateful bastard!". Sony became guilty; arrogance was a good trait in a championship, but not around his girlfriend. He rubbed her leg and looked at her with a sincerity that only she could bring out of him. "Go on; I want to learn". Her face returned to normality (sensing Sony's innocence). "Alright then, let's get closer to the water". The couple got up and travelled to the fresh, running water, carrying their provisions with them. Sony sat down but Linda bent over and picked up the tea ladle, whisk, pot and the bowls. Sony watched her intently as she crouched next to the water and began scooping it into her hands, rubbing it with a circular motion around the equipment; her eye shot was focused and unchanging (not even blinking) as if there was nothing there; like her soul had left. She returned with the cleansed tools and sat eye to eye with Sony; leaving a small gap between them as she sat on her knees with her back perfectly straight and her bum rested on her feet (this part Sony recognised: basic Japanese seating position). They sat in complete silence as she took the wooden chips, lying them on the floor. She then took the pot and opened the lid to reveal the water which by then was distinctively marked by the floating tea she was pouring into it. She then lade tissue on the wooden chips and put the pot on top of it before setting fire to the boiling tea with a lighter and placing the lid on the pot. The feeling was ultra-surreal to Sony; it was as if there was a presence. As the tea brewed, Linda looked at Sony, "before we drink, take twenty breaths through the nose and out through the mouth. Count each breath and close your eyes". Sony waited to enquire but Linda's eyes were already closed and her breathing had begun: she was like a stone; still and perfect. But Sony couldn't focus his mind; he was moving through a thousand thoughts and the only thing he could focus on was Linda's chest; (moving up and down, her perfect breast raising and lowering slowly) his mind was only focused by the sensation in his trousers. She awoke from her breath circulation and poured the tea into the cups, handing one to Sony and keeping one for herself. Even with this her focus was immaculate and the ladle moved with an air and grace that did not shake and as Sony sure the tea move into the cups it never splashed and moved in one direction; never wavering. She explained: "before you drink, first bow then raise the cup and then turn it". Sony nodded and Linda stood up and bowed to commence the procedure. She then drank half of the tea and extended it to Sony (who followed the procedure). The tea entered his body smoothly and his senses immediately calmed as though he had just walked out from a massage. He also felt that his senses were heightened: he could feel the wind and water (that was nowhere near him) as though it was washing across his skin. He looked at the cup intently and saw calligraphy scattered in green paint across the white ceramic. He bowed and passed the cup back to Linda (their hands touched softly) and Sony fell into shock; thrown into an emptiness he could not describe, he and Linda were surrounded by sunlight and he could see her outline: it was black and the ritual flashed in chronological order (in the space of two minutes). "You feel it don't you" Linda said (breaking the vision). "What..... "You'll understand soon. Come on; we have to go".

Caribbean music was playing; Bob Marley: no woman no cry. His soulful voice mellowed the bar. It was a humid night and the smell of marijuana surrounded Linda and Sony outside. They were sitting on wooden chairs around a circular table with a group of Linda's friends; (mostly musicians and Jamaicans) naturally she was smoking a joint and the air was sweet with the smell of white rum. Everyone was merry and there were groups of people huddled around; some playing guitars, some the flute and some just passing a bong amongst each other. Sony was enjoying himself (although it was not his usual scene); he enjoyed the peacefulness and cultural diversity of the tiki bar in London. He had forgotten most of the day and the night had called him to party with the best looking girl in Croydon and a bottle of Wray Nephews by his side (this was the first time in years that he had enjoyed himself). Of course he loved the thrill of fighting and the personal magnitude of the quest that gave him purpose in life but everyone has to 'chillax' sometime. And then a voice came from inside; calling Linda: "hey! Baby girl. You up next man". They looked around and sure the Cuban club owner; a chubby and bubbly character dressed in a blue blazer with a white t shirt underneath and a gold chain. Linda led the way in and Sony staggered behind her. She walked through the pathway surrounded by tables and Sofas broken up by plastic palm streets and the orange, purple and blue lighting from the ceiling (coupled with loud music) which made Sony dizzy. But he endured just long enough to find a brown leather sofa at the side of the bar; quite close to the stage where Linda was standing beside the owner (she looked beautiful in her multi coloured long dress patterned like an Arabian carpet). "Hello! Hello! Hello! Everybody. I hope you lots is having a good time!" Said the owner in his strong, South American accent. "Now as our special guest line up we have one of the most famous poets from Croydon!....called by the National association of poets 'the most competent poet of the next generation! Miss Linda Ranjit!" The crowd whistled and applauded her immensely (she was a true icon in multicultural London and a true statement of a changing generation). The introduction brought it all back to Sony and (when they were with each other they often forgot each other's individualism) his memory gathering gave him great pride (partly spurred on by the emotions that alcohol usually invoked in him). The applauding chorus continued and Linda began to break it: "thank you! Thank you everyone! I love each and every one of you; without you guys, none of this would be possible. Today I've got something special for you. This piece of work was inspired by my love for a special man; the day we met was the day my life started. It's called 'Green tea'. Sony was ridiculously happy inside; he was physically struggling to control himself but he giggled inside; a result of the huge cauldron of feelings that were involved (not least of which was the cuteness he found in the high-ness which he could clearly hear in her voice). He braced himself and began to stabilise his drunkenness; all for this moment.

Our love is a forked path,
It goes two ways but is joined at the start,
Believe me when I say this is my heart,
When we first sure each other, we we're both in the dark,
Now for me the light is here, this pen was the start,
It climbed with me,
And I don't think it comes naturally,
I used to be so angry,
But now I let it go, and it's all inside me,

Like you,
And now you need guidance, I don't know what to do,
When you touch me, you do it perfectly,
Like green it soothes me,
And now my pen is perfect,
But you're pen is not,
You gave me love,
But for your pen you have none,
I wish I could help,
But the only thing that can help is yourself,
Why my pen dries, I ask why,
Then I close my eyes and breath,
To find peace,
The only thing that can save you is in the green tea,
So you can feel perfect, like when you touch me.

Linda fell silent; breathing out slowly. A roar came from the audience and Sony was now levelled by the gravity laid upon him by the poem; it was powerful and the truth. The questions in his head scared him and she was the only one with any kind of answer. She got off the stage and ignored the swarms of fans lunging towards her and walking up she kissed Sony and sat next to him. "I love you" she whispered. Those three words embodied everything she felt (and Sony knew that) but the question was still in his head and it wouldn't leave: "I still don't understand: what does the green tea mean?" He finally asked. "Sony, I still don't know; all I can tell you is that its

Zen inspired". Sony was now unimpressed; whatever his answer was it wasn't in religion (that is a myth and the only truth is strength).

CHAPTER 4: WILLIAM'S POWER

"My art is different from yours: it consists not in defeating others but in not being defeated"
-Tsukhara Bokuden, Samurai saint

The black taxi pulled up outside the Redhill vineyard. It had passed through the sloping stone and concrete path; going through young apple trees (giving fruition to bright red English countryside fruit) alongside bright green bushes with cup shaped leaves. The driver respectfully takes his money and drives of. William and Madam Louise are now standing at the top of the vineyard; stretching their limbs from the peaceful sleep they had on the ride up (finally over the alcohol from the previous night). They widened their eye shots to the surrounding area; the trees of the encapsulating forests give a true sense of a magnificent, free land as they tower in the distance (light and fluffy like bunches of hair. Yellowish and dark green in complexion). The skies above them have a hole in it circled by white clouds on a hot summer's day. He crossed his arms and turned to her, "good enough?" She starts to walk ahead, "just about". They walked further up the top until they found a conventionally stationed, rectangular wooden guest house with a welcoming extended gazette at the front supported by wooden columns; underneath it where bright white and yellow canopies mounted on sticks providing shade for small tables (a perfect cultural antidote for the vineyard housing the finest English sparkling wine). But there would be time for that later; for now it was time to see the grapes that would provide them with this treat. They walked past the house and downhill towards the rows of grape vines. William wrapped his arm around the madam and straightened his back walking proudly with her. She was wearing a skirt designed with overlapping strips at the bottom of the Spanish design; flamboyant in its red tone and her top had similar strip decorations around the V shaped collar stretching about halfway on her body (cream coloured and made from silk). Her jet black hair is tied back and (although she is not dressed in the conventional style of her class) there is an heiress about her that screams nobility. "You look divine today sweat heart" William said; (beginning a conversation that he knows won't stop) usually he wasn't in the mood for talking but today was a 'treat', so he felt obliged to make an exception. "Don't I always?" She sarcastically remarks. "For god sake. Can't you just take a compliment without being mouthy about it?!" "No! You remind me of dad: always making pointless comments for the sake of it". "Wow! That's something I thought I'd never hear you accuse me of: measuring up to the great Lord Adam (the almighty architect of Great Britain)". Louise stopped in her tracks and went in his face. "Listen, I'm only going to say this once: do....not.....talk about my father. I wasn't comparing in anyway; he was a pioneer in the industry. He designed the most competent structure of towns (shaping the way our towns are built today). What have you ever shaped; a fat lip?" William's facial expression didn't change; he looked just as calm, collected and continued: "when was that again? 1946 right. Funny that; it was my uncle who proposed the new towns act to the government". She was now becoming agitated and grabs him, swinging him around. "So what!!" "So... Your dad wouldn't have 'pioneered' anything if it wasn't for my uncle. Actually, (come to think of it) doesn't that mean you wouldn't have a job; I mean, the only reason you got to be a journalist was of his back wasn't it?" A firm backhand suddenly struck William across his face; moving him sideways dramatically. "Ok, I deserved that".

"Yes...You...Did. My success is of my own back and..." "Ok, OK, I know: free independent woman and all that crap (I didn't start this argument). Can we just get back to the whole point of this day". William pointed to the left and Louise looked across to the long stretch of vineyards in long rows running up another curved hill of grassland; the wooden poles enshrined with flattened leaves bearing a wide surface, light green with a fresh colouring (bunched together to create bushes). Next to the rows are a pathway decorated with tiny, powdered, blue flowers bearing shiny stems and narrow leaves. The couple walk hand in hand; admiring the grounds of their valued drinking pass time and in minutes all was forgotten. They stroll the whole field; passing tall trees and the lake in the centre (which itself has a purple border of nature's pollen attractions). They passed various creatures and insects: from pestering wasps to the adorable squirrels. All the while they entertained each other (their volatile relationship's friendly banter precedent of course). After two hours they returned to the gazette house, ready to indulge in the substance both were craving in the back of their minds. They sat on the small table together with a fresh bottle of sparkling wine (famed in the vineyard's reputation) and indeed Britain's rural setting had a humbling glory around it; its small umbrellas and oak tree tables marking its authenticity. They begin to drink the yellowish liquid. As William slurps, he notes the transparent bubbles (the trademark of this national pride). It was sweet and fruity like a ripened green gage; the grape flavour was distinct and it's reflection in the sunlight was almost magical. It inspired a thought inside the man's head: "sometimes I have to question our species; nature provides such glory yet we scheme our human ambitions to rewrite it (and my job is definitely the pinnacle of this obsession). Nature is the greatest architect". "But isn't our ambition an inspiration from nature; are we not it's pinnacle?" Critiqued Louise. He smiles. "You always have an answer for my question. The developer and the thinker. Great stuff", "traits of a journalist my love", "I still remember the day you answered the question of my love". Louise smiled with real sincerity (it was a look William was unaccustomed to). "So typical, isn't it? We meet at the biggest town innovation in Croydon. I still remember you in your nerdy grey suit and bow tie. Even through all that lack of dress sense I could still see the shape of a successful man". William snickered and stretched his jaw into a charismatic snarl. "And even through that common sense of style I could see that ruthless edge that would shape one of the Sun's best editors. Who would have thought it: the Whitgift opening event (through sheer chance) would bring a town developer and a journalist together". "Well not exactly luck my dear: you were looking at designs for inspiration and I was writing about an inspiring design; we both needed each other: business breeds contacts", "even so; total clash", "I agree. But what a wonderful one". Louise ended with softness in her voice that would only ever grace William's ear. They then finished a second bottle and ordered a cab to fill the appetite which only drink could have given them.

The menu looked enticing. I mean say what you want about the size of Redhill town: it may be smaller than the other commercial centres in London but their Toby cavern was one of the best around (or at least that's what William and Louise thought). The decor of an expensive inn styled restaurant, good staff and a more than decent salad bar, the patterned carpet and the vintage style darkened furniture helped to make it as intimate as could be (and obviously their own VIP section helped). As William held the menu in his hand he felt the need to entertain some small talk: "I sure Rebecca yesterday", "is it? How is she?", "same as always: so stuck up her own ass her neck's double jointed", "being a proud woman doesn't mean you're stuck up your own ass William", "she's not proud, she's a lesbian; all that feminist crap", "feminist crap! Listen you chauvinistic fool, us women are twice as competent in every respect as you men and it's about time your sex realised that. Things are changing: finally we're moving past the disease of these century old stereotypes". "And what decease is that? Reality". Louise leaned back on her chair and crossed her legs underneath the table. "Well it can't be reality mate. I hear that the government's thinking about 'refurbishing' the equal pay act", "and let me guess, you heard that from Rebecca?" He responded (with a raised eyebrow). "Hey, she's a reliable source. I mean she is connected to Parliament". As soon as she finished her sentence a young woman with a small notebook and pen (wearing a white shirt and apron) strolled up to the couple. "So how's our celebrating pair? What would you like?" Louise pulled herself away from the debate to cut William before he began to talk: "we're great thanks. I'll have a honey and mustard glazed Salmon with asparagus and he'll have a salmon fillet with chips". "Thanks, and drinks?" "You're most expensive bottle of red wine please". "Excellent. We'll be with you shortly". William flashed the waitress an artificial grin and she strolled of. He turned his attention back to Louise. "So; I really would like to know where you picked up that skill", "what skill?" "Mind reading!" "Oh! I don't need a skill to do that (you're just boring)". William laughed and rolled his eyes. "Well anyway (going back to the matter at hand) I don't think you can tell me that the assistant to the assistant of New Addington's councillor is a reliable source". "Why not? She speaks directly to Mary Walker". "Well forgive me babe but she's not exactly a senior MP now is she?" "She beat three men; she's obviously doing something right" she shrugged. As William was about to begin his rebuttal she raised her hand. "I don't want to speak about this anymore. The last thing I'm going to say is that you should mark my words: we'll soon see a female prime minister in this country". William's facial expression became disheartened. "Ok. We'll see". The young waitress returned to their table; this time with a serviette bearing a bottle of Rochetto Mascarello with a bright red Italian title on it. The waitress unscrewed the cap and poured the dark red wine into the cups; (whilst assuring the couple that their food was coming soon) as it poured the distinct smoothness was of great satisfaction to the couple and Louise was even licking her lips. She began to drink. William waited patiently for her to put down her glass. "Well whatever your views, I definitely admire your sex's determination". As he began to reach for his glass Louise sure the rough skin on his knuckles (noting the unnatural extension of them), reached over and rubbed. "I'm not the only one with determination. You better win that tournament; I don't wanna be with a loser (especially when your opponents are a bunch of uncultured apes)". William smirked with admiration and downed his drink. "For a new age woman concerned with the idioms of the past you sure sound like an elitist", "come on now William don't be stupid; we're from the same class. We both know the inferiority of these uncivilised porpers (especially those

'Japs'). I don't get it: how did they develop such an advanced fighting style; the same victims of the A bomb". William was becoming unsettled; his closest friends were 'porpers' but they were different from the rest (nevertheless he felt compelled to come to their aid). "That's a bit harsh isn't it?" Louise sharpened her gaze and a very rare brow formed between her eyebrows. "William, I'm not a feminist because I believe in a socialist Britain. I'm a feminist because British women are a superior breed and we should not be treated like the coloured people. Look at this great land; once home to the greatest empire in the world. I remember my dad teaching me the best lessons of my childhood: the truth about the Labour bureaucrats and the end they were bringing to our British power. If the politicians don't respect our legacy then it's down to us (the elite of our communities) to prove we are the best. Be the best William, for all our sakes". The last few sentences rippled through William's heart; it was the softness that she ever spoke to him in all the years they knew each other. She was right: he was taught to be the best and he is the best, the elite. The thought carried the most expensive dinner with it; personally crafted by the chef to satisfaction and the young waitress placed it in front of the couple. They ate until the end of the night. It was only a usual 'treat' for the two; perhaps an embodiment of their own truths: even a date was the best of the best.

CHAPTER 5: ROGER'S NIGHT

'We are moral beings, we are not to lower ourselves to the status of animality. What is the use of becoming a fine swordsman if he loses his human dignity?'
-Odagari Ichiun, master of 'The sword of the no-mind' school

Roger's hand was on the steering wheel. His grip was strong and firm but only due to complacency; behind it he was tired (caused more by his mundane mental state of another boring day at work than physical exertion). He drives the yellow Austin martin to the side of the road outside the block of flats in Thornton Heath where standing outside of the old building was Kate wearing a leather mini skirt and a matching leather waist jacket that exposed a low cut top; it was a street slick look and one that Roger loved (her clean cut frame and sharp European features gave her the qualities needed to pull of this style). Naturally large breasts and a perfectly round bum gave him great pride to hold such a radiant lady amongst the trash that the district usually gave birth to (in his experience). Kate walked towards the small car; its square design with a rectangular front part was her ticket to the world; and inside was the man who would carry her. She opened the door and bursts in with excitement. "Ready for the night" Roger asked with a slight nod(his version of an exciting gesture), "let's drive babes" she responded. Roger pulled the car up on Thornton Heath high street and the couple left it outside the height of Thornton Heath's class; built like a horizontal, three step pyramid with two, dark brick bordering steps with vertically running windows. The front face of the building was separated by three long strips running down it in a modern Coliseum architectural style (reflective of the classic London mark on the area). As they approached the building they entered the doors on the left which had the sign above it: 'The Granada cinema'. They looked at the bill board for the film times and both realised they had no idea of what they were going to watch; so (doing the courteous thing) Roger followed tradition: "what should we see?" Kate looked up to the ceiling for a moment. "Ummm.... Let's watch Rocky two". Roger was relieved. "You sure?" "Yeh; Sylvester Stallone bear chested, great stuff", "ha....ha....ha. That's not a chest" Roger joked. She then rubbed his chest in a brushing motion. "Don't I know it". And with that they went in and sat at the back of the cinema. It was ten o' clock and the cinema was almost bear. "Perfect", she thought. The two stayed cuddled together throughout the movie and they were both zoned into the life story of the boxing icon: Roger was focused on the struggle of the champion embodied by Silvester Silone; the struggle of a natural born contender whose life was incomplete without boxing and the future challenges faced by having a spouse whilst still living the solitary life of a fighter (marked by pain and the butterfly effect it had on those he loved). The ring champion's setbacks caused by poverty resonated with him and the need to become someone by physical means. It made him believe he could conquer the odds and was a source of inspiration for him. Meanwhile, Kate felt the same way but as the movie progressed, her constant strain of shaping the film star into the hero she was with (in her eyes) stirred her sexual appetite and brought back the day they met. She climbed into his lap and lurched her back against him; shutting her eyes and clasping their hands together (purposely applying gravity and using it to twist her body against him): a snake wrapping around its prey. This peaked towards the end of the film when Rocky was pounding Creed into the corner of the ring; spurred on by the words of his coach Mickey: "you're a tank, a greasy, fast Italian tank. Go get him!" That single sentence agitated the parts between her legs; forcing her to grip the memory.

It was William's birthday and the boys had travelled to West end to enter the delights of the first ever Playboy club in Park lane. The place was budding with city slick geezars with an eye for the luscious bunny girls in their brand recognised clothing. Sony and William were blowing money at one of the many roulette tables; spinning the gamblers circle and the tables with the lucky fella's squared numbers. The American style look gave the place a Las Vegas feel: the exotic plants, carpeted stairs, wooded banisters and small tables of gentlemen being served by stunning waitresses. Roger was sitting at the bar having a drink to cool the nerves (spurred on by the high risk stakes); sitting at a table at the back (shrouded in darkness). The smooth and seductive sounds of the RNB slow jam Atlantic star, was playing.

And now five years on she was whispering the lyrics in his ear. "Do you remember?" She hissed and he took the travel in time with her.

To when he grabbed her in intoxication. From the moment he sure her (in the bunny outfit) he noted she was leaning against the wall; tired from her shift and just taking a breath to pull herself together. He went up to her and took her hand and she was instantly attached to him; the built figure of his body compelled her to relinquish her duty and roll into his arms in the same position they were in now. They climaxed emotionally on the moment and awoke in a light headed daze. He was love struck and she was intoxicated by aching passion.

They left the cinema and entered the car (both of them thrilled from the epic they had just viewed). As they began to strap in their seat belts Kate suddenly jerked "shit! I left my pay check at the bar". Roger took a deep breath out in frustration; he wanted to end the night and rest with her (but alas it appeared the day would not end yet). "Well then; we better go get it". They drove through Whitehorse lane on the straight roads towards the town centre; passing the front entrance of the Whitgift shopping centre and zooming under the Croydon underpass, bending round to head in the direction of South Croydon. On their way they passed the immigration office. Roger's mood changed from annoyance to acceptance and he pointed towards the capital's sign of Croydon's otherwise country inclusion. "Remember that?" He said (keeping his yes on the road). "How could I forget?

Nineteen seventy one. Roger was marching with a few campaigners from the Labour ward of Thornton Heath (as well as Sony obviously) to protest against the Immigration act; which had restricted his cousin from claiming asylum. He was intrinsically angry (not at the law but as a side effect of his fear for his Jamaican cousin's fate; on the run from bounty hunters in Kingston). But as he and the others marched in proudly they sure two well-built police officers dragging a blonde haired girl with cuts on her face; crying desperately and ranting "pleases" and "listen to me". Roger recognised the voice vaguely and as the police officers walked towards them he looked down at the damsel to see the ruined features of the princess he unshivarlessly courted at the Playboy club a few months ago. The moment robbed him of his senses and blinded by rage he slammed his knee into the officers stomach and strategically thrusting his elbow in the top of the man's head whilst he was falling he knocked him into unconsciousness (with such a speed that it left the second officer in as much shock as the protesters were). But within a moment everyone snapped back to attention. As the officer drew his cosh Sony went under his shoulder and locked his arm whilst kicking off the ground (throwing his back against the man); curling him around his centre of gravity to roll him on the floor, smacking the man's head into a wall whilst rolling of off it. At this point the protesters had dispersed and Roger was in the car with Kate (ready to escape the sentence they would both face). Sony ran and jumped in. They were all panicking except for Kate (who although acting the part was actually excited). Once they reached safety in Addiscombe she explained the story which became the foundation of their relationship: how her family threatened to kill her if she didn't sleep with the immigration officers they were in touch with to smuggle cocaine into the country.

Now they were speeding down the route leading to Purley. Roger's foot was released on the clutch (it was his attempt to take the weight of anger of his mind). He swore he would never let a man touch her ever again and dammit, he would keep the promise. But as Kate stared at the windows and shops, houses and pubs began to dissolve into lines of colours; rapidly changing and coinciding with the sound of the car's engine. Her heart was racing, beating from the lie that she had just told; the one that would see blood on the streets of Coulsdon. She smiled at him (her eyes if he could have seen through the lens were cracked: shattered with the desire to control). She was not in love with him; she was in love with his strength, she was in love with the power. Without it she was nothing and she hung on it with everything inside her. Her nickers began to dampen, it was that, that turned her on (her lust for strength). Past the semi-rural district of Purley and coursing in to the deeper outskirts of Croydon. It was a fun journey during the day; the outskirts of the forest borders with farmlands and Gregorian houses marked the best of English countryside (a true testament to Croydon's surrey connection) but during the desolate nights it felt hazardous, like the classic scene of a stalker. They finally drove past Smitham rail station and were in the tiny development of Coulsdon. Inside Kate was gleeing with excitement. Roger was simply relieved.He began to slow down as they reached the small bar; it had no sign on it and was a small enterprise (but in an area such as Coulsdon it was able to gather a small community following that kept it out of recession). He turned the wheel and swerved into the side of the road when (at the point he was about to turn the key to turn the car of) he sure a shadow beside the company van he was parked behind. The van was white and stood out in the barren road; it had the label of the wholesalers printed in gold at the back: 'Robert and son's beverages' (it automatically clicked that it must be the bar's suppliers). Roger watched intently; making no changes to the car's current position. The man walked further onto the pavement and into the orangey street light. He began to bend down and pick up a long, shiny, black bag of metal with a curve at the end ('crowbar' he thought). He kept himself calm and collected turning to Kate "do you know that guy?" But when he looked at her she was paralysed and the only sign that she wasn't a zombie was a single tear rolling down her face. Calm turned to sharp concern that only the hurt of a loved one could bring. He grabbed her shoulder. "Kate, who is it?" She stammered to form the word and mumbled with a whisper: "cousin". And that was it: Roger disappeared within seconds (but Kate sure every move). He chopped the man in a pressure point above his collar bone, cutting the blood circulation long enough for Roger to drag the man in a headlock; throwing him into the back of the car. Since the door was 'fearlessly' opened by Kate he flew head first and slightly bounced of the door at the other end (only to bounce back into the door Roger closed). Roger glanced left and right (checking no one was there) but peering behind the corner of a road behind a house was another man (that looked quite similar to the one now in the back of the car). As soon as they made eye contact the head flew back and Roger was focused enough to hear the frantic footsteps. "Fucking cunt!" He shouted; racing into the car he jumped in and sped to the end of the road (spinning the car around the corner) but by then the man had vanished. Frustration ignited him. "Don't worry bitch: I don't forget a face and Croydon's a small place". His head spun to the skinny man in the back of the car wearing a black labourer's jump suit with leather gloves (that were holding his head). The man was clearly confused and was spatting Polish words. "Your boy was lucky but I'm just goanna have to take it out on you". He crookedly smirked at him and then turned to Kate with an unchanging expression. "Dear, give us a minute please". Kate looked like she was in a daydream and stepped out of the car but as she left she began sliding her tongue across her lips. She closed the door. Roger didn't say a word; he simply shoved his foot into the man's chest to secure him and removed his gloves hastily putting them on his hands. He couldn't wait to get started. From then on it was a massacre: his hands slammed all over the man's face and with each blow the rage was growing. The punches smashed against his nose; (breaking it) splattering his blood. The assault began to dent cheek bones and his knee was deep inside the man's stomach (wounding him to the point where the man had to many leaking openings of blood to count). Roger's madness exploded and he clutched the man's face with an open hand and began to slam it against the side of the door; back and front, back and forth. He decided he should kill him. But in the moment his mind moved towards picking up the crowbar on the pavement the man croaked "please". That simple word returned Roger's humanity to him (he felt something eating away at him).

Whilst this was happening Kate was watching from outside. The sadistic woman becoming wetter by the minute; turned on by the sight of blood and the control she was emanating. "He should have never tried to cross me" she told herself whilst reaching for her arm; feeling the burn marks that she received. "Look at what they've made me. Look at what i've become" she thought; remembering her hay day as the masseuse that became a male pimp (commanding a small army of hardened Eastern European female gangsters who jumped to her whims). Seeing (at the age of ten) the torture of her liberal mother to the hands of fascist police officers she swore that she would never fall beneath the feet of a man and that was exactly what happened. She kidnapped and prostituted the wrong Russian and he exacted his revenge: escaping from the confines of her East London business to assemble his anti-communist asylum brothers (who sure fit to brand her and use her as their leverage ticket to foreign office security). It was only by an odd chance of fate that Roger (the man she met on one of her mule running's to one of the prostitute lords at Hugh Heffner's enterprise) saved her. Now she had to rebuild; but she needed a weapon and she definitely found one in Roger. She warmed to the man, they were similar; both oppressed, both seeking something better. She had convinced herself they were good partners; it was what every partnership needed: a brain and a brawn (to her that was love).

Roger threw the man out of the car; crying and near dead behind a wall nearby. Kate entered (fully satisfied with every moment of the event she had just caused). He drove back with his jacket in the back of the car covered in blood and his hands stained with it. Kate was happy but her partner wasn't (it unease's her mood). "Are you ok.....He didn't hurt you did he?" Roger didn't look at her; he purposely kept his vision centred (and Kate could tell). "It isn't that" he said (it was as though he didn't want to talk). "Well; what is it?" Responded Kate (pretending to be sympathetic towards his feelings). "I lost control: I was goanna kill that guy Kate. That's not the way; it's not Bushido". His voice was shaky (the first time Kate had heard it like that) and she didn't like it one bit. "Learning to fight is about protecting the one's you love isn't it and being the best at that?" "Yes but with control", "but how can you be the best if you're controlled?" She touched the blood stained hand on the steering wheel. "To be the best Roger you can't be; (in self-defence or championships) you do what you need to win, to be the best. You can't let your emotions rule you. To be the best you can't be disciplined because control creates limits and someone who challenges you doesn't deserve limits; you have to get through them (that makes the fight limitless if you really want the end goal)". Roger was now confused; Kate had contradicted his whole outlook. He knew he was a hot head but he always thought he should have limits. But if those limits stopped him, what was the point? He was going to be entering the greatest tournament in his life; fighters would come from all parts of the country. They all knew what they were getting themselves into, they all wanted what he wanted (and he knew from the experiences of generations before him that some would hate him to have it because of the colour of his skin) therefore they are all enemies. Kate looked at him and smiled to comfort him; she may have not been capable of true love but she understood it: she understood her words carried the weight of a thousand actions and she knew he would listen and believe. Her answer was reasonable; the best lie always has some truth in it.

CHAPTER 6: A DAY OF MARTIAL PRIDE

At the headquarters of Greenwhich Leisure Limited, (in the prestigious borough of Greenwhich) in Middlegate house at the royal arsenal the staff were running around like headless chickens; phones ringing and conversations buzzing through the offices as they prepared for one of the most glorious martial art events in the country.

Inside the leisure centre five thousand retractable seats were being put up and the sports hall was receiving a thorough mop in the early hours of the morning; making the floors shine intensely (it's pale brown colours clashed distinctively with the blue seating). The staff began to lay large, square, blue mats until the entire floor was covered. The manager looked from the back of the hall and proudly watched the organisation of the long venue (it had the perfect width and a rectangular length that stretched as though it was a field merged with a Coliseum). The venue was spick and span: from the descending chairs to the high wooden roof above it. All of the attractions, chairman, referees and judges had arrived. It was truly a day of martial pride.

To the far left of the hall was the Iado and Kendo practitioners with wooden swords (dressed in armour) circling the master slicing down on to a loath of bread and stopping it with immaculate control just before landing to then harness his Ki energy: blasting it through the loaf and blowing up the brick beneath it. The building was alight with culture: Japanese dancers rehearsed on the mats (with their graceful fan sequences) as well as the Judo league coming to demonstrate their throwing potential. It would be a community day full of excitement. At the sides of the hall at the centre were the tables for the masters and three tables in front of the stage for the greatest fighters in the country. But this was not an exclusively British day: various supporters from other nations had also come; from American Jujitsu masters, to superstars of the warrior world. This tournament was a display of Britain's martial spirit. It was a time for business, celebration and competition.

As the time drew closer for the grand opening everyone took their positions for centre stage until Ten PM sure the floods of competitors, friends and families rush through the door. Mums, dads, children, local councillors and pioneers of the oriental fighting arts took their seating and created the atmosphere of a diverse and wonderful day. Conversation was bustling in the hall and on the mats were hundreds of Kyokushinkai students (of all grades and levels) talking amongst each other and tying their belts. The head of the British Kyokushinkai league stood at the far left of the hall on a raised platform; dressed in a blue suit and Cimac trainers (a slim individual but his impeccable posture demonstrated a clear confidence that noted his power). He was an eighth degree black belt (the highest possible rank for a Kyokushinkai practitioner outside of Japan) and to his left and right stationed bellow him were his deputy and the chairman (both carried the same attire and resonating aura). The chairman turns towards the rows of students and shouts "attention!" The students snapped into discipline and began to perfect the ranks; with black belts at the front and white belts at the back. "Ready!" He shouts and both aids walk in front of the master; entering the Shizen Tai (ready stance). Behind the master was a large Kyokushinkai flag with the symbols on it in Japanese calligraphy. "Bow to the flag!" The man shouts and snapping his feet together he bows (followed by a simultaneous bow from all the students in the hall). "Bow to the Sensei!" (Again the process was repeated) The Sensei returned the bow and the other two turned to face the crowds and the master began to officially open the day.

The whole room was silent. "Origato students! I am pleased to see all of you here today in another year of celebration of our great art. This year's Kyokushinkai knockdown tournament is heading towards a great day where we can all test our will, determination and the spirit of Osu. We thank each and every one of you here today for supporting our event: friends, families, communities and sponsors. There are a range of activities for everyone to enjoy and we hope you take the opportunity to take a look at all of them. We've broken our programme down into three sections: the first will be a socialising time for everyone to communicate, get to know each other and try everything out. This will finish at noon and will be followed by a one hour lunch break were everyone can get drinks, food and other refreshments. We will then begin the competition stages amongst the lower grades up to brown belt; mat one will be the Kata (performance/sequence) tournament, mat two will be the breaking tournament and mat three will be the sparring tournament. This will then conclude with a fifteen minute break and then the Black Belt and Dan tournaments will begin; after which we will rap up and end the day. I wish you all the very best of luck and I hope your Osu gives you victory". The chairman and deputy led the final bow and the students cleared the mats whilst the other attractions took centre stage.

CHAPTER 7: WILLIAM'S ARRIVAL

"To know and to act are one and the same"
-Mas Oyama, the founder of Kyokushinkai karate

William arrived to the tournament late. He pulls up in his white Porsche: sliding into the parking space (conveniently stationed near the sports centre). Louise was with him and the couple had left the car; holding each other proudly. His Gi(uniform) was freshly pressed and bright white with the black belt tied to perfection and (although these pretences kept the public convinced) as William took each step towards the building his heart began to beat faster. The pair walked through the doors and into the hall. As he strode through he was greeted by various fighters. He first bowed to his master (who he diligently went to find) out of respect.

He was standing beside the other masters commencing conversations; from idol chat about their personal lives in regards to their children and jobs (discussing in the comfort of old friends brought together). William stood there as the old masters talked; (their words carried a martial weight unseen in the current generations of fighters) these were pioneers and veterans accustomed and born out of a decade of revolution and real fighting spirit. However, conversation began to turn into educated debate (as they relived stories of a day and age of giants). William's master kicks it off: "hey Nick, how's those fellas from Hawaii; still breeding Samurai?" A tall African American man with a shaped Afro and skinny but refined physique turned in response. "Yeah they're alright from what I've heard. Professor Okazaki's getting a bit old though; Kufferath is more in charge now. But you know what? Those Judo guys are really turning out to be something". William's master gives a sincere grin and releases his hand in gest. "Well that's no surprise;

(especially when the founder raised the students there) good old Jigaro Kano; i'll never forget the day I trained there (you don't get Judo like that anymore)". The other masters turned from there other discussions to grunt in agreement whilst William nodded his head respectfully. His master turned to him and gave another smirk to the crowd of masters (but there was a sly implication this time). He smacked William on the back "so William, who do you think stands a chance this year (see anyone who might be competition)? William turned to his master with undivided attention; embarrassed in front of the experienced audience. "Not really sensei. You should know anyway (after all you're the one who taught us)". The master gives a bellowing laugh of appreciation and modesty. "Yes Will; that I did. I make it a point to train the best (I mean Croydon does have the finest squad)". The masters began to become uneasy and one short but very stocky Russian gentlemen named master George folded his arms and returned a condescending grin. "Well they're all over there" he said; pointing. "I'm sure every part of the country has something to other. You remember Samuel and Curtis don't you Will?" William took his first glance at the gathering of twenty fighters. "Yes! We haven't trained since that summer camp. It must be about ten years since I've seen them". "Yeah, you should go and catch up (size up the competition)". Both masters gave William an open smile (it was all guest to them; competitive friendship). So he nodded to the masters and made his way other to the group. Louise was sitting comfortably (in her usual cold manner).

In the circle of Dan students there was one particularly tanned gentleman who was quite colossal in structure with a bald head. But as William neared, his features were clearly recognisable: 'Joey Santez' he thought and stood in front of the man. "Alright geezar!" He shouted with an open, childlike body expression. The man looked down at William (without changing his facial expression). His features were broad and exasperated as he extended his right hand and shook William's. "It's been a long time my old friend!" The deep voice responded. The man's face was unscathed but hardened (unmistakeably the training of a decade). As soon as the first man spoke to William a whole flurry of other black belts began to reintroduce themselves from childhood. One man in the group with a wild, crazy hairstyle and a head which appeared smaller than his already skeletal body began to talk. "You good mate; (It's been ages) how's the school going?" "It's good yunno: the last few years have seen a considerably higher levels of interest" William answered. "Well it's a changing country mate; martial arts have taken off. Are you sure your chapys are up to the challenge? We're reaching for world fame here". The comment bit into William's mind (making it wheezy) and what made the comment even more poignant was the commentator: David Major; famed in Nottingham and throughout the midlands for his diligence in breaking and known for his speed in competition. Even so, every man must fight his corner: "well believe in me: we're definitely up for being number one and you'll see that later on today". With that he quickly excused himself to talk with his girlfriend; of whom was still sitting by herself in the background (now pouting in neglect).

William sat next to her and stretched his arm over her shoulder. She rested her head on his chest and felt his heart beating rapidly. She lifted her head and sat more conventionally in a kind of back to business look. "So when are you fighting?" She asked. "Later on in the programme; after the less senior students". Louise was about to enter a full discussion when the sight of Roger and Kate walking through the doors of the hall entered the corner of her eye. By the looks of it the couple had just spotted them (as they were walking speedily towards the two). Kate was walking awkwardly whilst Roger seemed overly relieved (with a pumped out chest). They eventually reached their destination; standing in front of William and Louise with Kate wrapped around Roger's body. She sprung up and awkwardly placed herself between the pair. "Hi love birds. It's nice to have all of us here today". She then turned her attention to William. "You must be excited? I plan to see you with at least a silver Mr (because obviously Roger has to get the gold)". At that point Roger walked over and sat next to William complacently. "Well babes we'll have to see about that" he said whilst nudging William. "Indeed ladies and whilst we excuse ourselves to check out the competition I advise that you take a look around (we'll be with you shortly)". With that excuse the men left the women to join the other black belts. Roger found a similar welcome to William's and then the banter started; initiated by Joey Santez: "so Roger, what's your game plan; how do you plan to get through us then?" Roger clenched his fist (to show the bulkiness of his knuckles). "Not me Santez; this: it can go through anything and God save the man who tries to stop it", "oh! Is that so? Well I've gone through plenty in my time as well Roger (so don't expect any mercy from me)". Roger cut his eye at the man. "Well (as it happens) I don't think I'm John Walker: you won't break my leg mate. But as old friends we make a pact: if we fight each other there is no mercy". Roger thrusted his hand forward for the handshake; a contract and Joey sealed the agreement. "Only for the weak my old friend". At that point David Major decided to take the stage: "I'm the best in the country and (today on the mat) I'll prove it. I was born for this". He said; hoping to insight William's anger but he received a sarcastic cover up instead as William turned to Roger. "We'll definitely see what the countryside's taught you but let's wait; for now I wanna hear about your epic victories in San Francisco". With that the conversation changed. Although these men were not masters all twenty were experienced fighters and as such they did what all men of youth but considerable experience did: they interchanged and swapped stories with each other; from the various loose women and continental diversities in the opposite gender, to their meetings at mountain temples with renowned masters. Hailing the fetes of courage some demonstrated against underground gangs in Hong Kong and the Oriental legacies passed on to US military bases in Malaysia (if one was to sit and listen to the tales they could in fat write a story far superior than this one).

Meanwhile the two women were sitting with each other. Although the two had seen each other frequently over the years they still considered each other friendly acquaintances. Kate began the conversation: "you must be as anxious as I am? I could swear i'm more exited for Roger than he is for himself". Louise looks back to Kate with a relaxed gaze, "off course you are; (we've been waiting for so long) they're finally goanna get to prove themselves. After today's said and done I'm just looking forward to eating dinner with a champion (I swear I'll probably dump him if he loses)". Kate's facial expression was confused with a slight hint of agitation. "Well we know they're not going to lose and (besides) I'm not looking forward to eating my dinner's underneath the sheets when we get back". The two looked at each other with childish expressions (like two teenage girls whispering to each other at school). Louise's eyebrow moved up. "And I suppose that's why you're having trouble walking today?" Kate closed her legs and put her hands on her knees whilst making her eyebrows flutter. "That's a girls prerogative isn't it?" She giggled underneath a tilted hand. "Well I feel we're digressing on a conversational road I'd rather not turn on. Let's play with some of the attractions on offer". The two women left their seats to take part. They went to the Kendo practitioners and were given an opportunity to learn some of the basic strikes with the wooden Boken sword. Kate was guesting throughout the 'learning experience' whilst Louise was stiff becoming frustrated when she couldn't get the hang of it. The two were paired up to train with each other but (to Louise's relief) she spotted someone on the mat next to there's; her long brown hair and light copper complexion made her stand out from the other dancers (whose faces were powdered white and lips bloodshot red); amongst the whirling clash of fans of the synchronised professionals and vein attempts of women from all ages and backgrounds simply waving the fans in vanity, the only thing that would have given Linda a chance of blending in was the similarity of her bright yellow and silver kimmino. Louise dragged Kate hastily to form the trio. "Hello you! What's all this then? (charitable support)" Louise tried to shout. Linda came of the mat and bowed. "Origato ladies!" she began (until facing interruption from Kate). "'Nd' same to you. I bet you keep Sony's attention with that foreplay" Linda winked; giving a naughty look to the girls. "Well that's for me to know and for us to gossip about". Louise sighed and rolled her eyes (to make herself the centre of attention). "Please people; were not at a sleep over (we're in public). And taking this conversation below the nine o' clock watershed: where's your better half?" "He's just been warming up at the back. Let's go get him". "I'll get the other two; hold on" said Kate. She bounced over to the group of black belts; tugging Roger and slapping William to get their attention.

The five walked with Linda; who took them to a corner of the sports hall where the changing rooms and toilets were. They stepped in to the dry surroundings of the changing room; (everything was untroubled) there were grey lockers on the green walls and a shower dominated one wall and a maze of changing cubicles blocked the centre view of the couples. Linda led them through to the centre (were Sony sat in nothing but a towel meditating). "Babes" Linda whispered whilst rubbing his shoulder. The man opened his eyes slowly and sure the couples standing next to each other. Roger had a smirk on his face. "So mate; the tournament's that stressful: I mean if you have to clear your mind, maybe you're not ready". Sony lazily looked up at Roger (not bothered by his remark). "I'm not preparing for the likes of you guys; I'm on stage soon". Louise looked at William. "On stage. On stage for what?" Sony's eyes sharpened on her. "To show people like you the extent of Kyokushinkai power" he said proudly. "And how's that then? (I wanna hear this one)". Sony noted the contempt in William's voice at the secret he had kept from his comrades. "Don't worry guys (it's far beneath you); just have to kick the crap out of fifty guys. No sweat". Sony stood on his feet to become level with everyone but (guessing from the expression on William's face) it looked like this betrayal could not go unnoticed. Roger interjected with a cool sentiment: "well mate, do us proud". He turned to William and calmly gestured to him. "The only guys he has to worry about is us; the rest aren't even in the equation". William accepted this point of view and he put his hand firmly on Sony's shoulder. "Just save your energy and Osu boy (you're goanna need it)." None of the women spoke and the couples departed; leaving Linda with Sony. "It's time now babe; they're clearing the stage for you". She kissed him softly and walked in front (leaving him with the solitude of his own beating heart as he dressed himself).

CHAPTER 8: SONY'S STAGE

'Even if it seems certain that you will lose, retaliate. Neither wisdom nor technique has a place in this. A real man does not think of victory or defeat. He plunges recklessly towards an irrational death. By doing this, you will awaken from your dreams'.
— Yamamoto Tsunetomo Hagakure, author of 'The Book of the Samurai'

He marched outside the changing room; opening the door to receive the daylight spread over the colourful arena (continuing to take the centre stage of the mat).
He turned his vision around the room to see the completely cleaned mats that were only stationed by the judges sitting in front of him on the tables. There were the rustling sounds and crying baby noises of an otherwise quite audience. Their eyes latched on to him; giving the surveillance presence that was necessary for the dramatization of the ceremony. On the mat (now standing next to him) was Dean Rodman; the most senior referee in the hall and a retired legend of Kyokushinkai. He was holding a foamed mike and breathed deeply through his nostrils to prepare for the announcement. "Good afternoon everyone! We hope and trust that you've enjoyed the many acts and activities we've had on display for you guys today. It is now time for us to present our special act, after which we will begin the lunch break. In Kyokusinkai (as many of you know) we pride ourselves on the Spirit of Osu instilled in our system; undoubtedly owed to the founder Mayata Oyama. Many of you will also know that our founder and grandmaster was the first man in recorded history to set up and complete the one hundred man knockdown tournament: fighting and defeating one hundred people consecutively in rounds of two minutes over a period of three days (nonstop). He was the only man for five years to ever complete the challenge. Today we would like to prove and demonstrate our teacher's legacy: by showing all of you for our centre stage finale: a fifty man Kumite(fight) we're our student Sony will compete against fifty black belts; following the same standards and traditions laid before us in the past. And

now without further ague".

He turned to face Sony. "Bow to the flag!" Sony turned and
bowed. "Bow to the Sensei's". Again he bowed. "Now bow
to your opponents". Sony gave the last bow to the fifty
black belts now standing around the mats; (touching side
to side like the single union of a roman legion) all in clean
and perfect uniforms with cotton strips wrapped around
their feet. They return the bow in union. The first man
steps on the mat towards Sony; who stamps forward with
his left leg into the mawashi dachi stance (extending his
left arm at shoulder level and diagonally descending his
right arm to waist level), both hands were opened. He felt
the solidness of the moment and the immense challenge
(following the man approaching him) who is now standing
a metre away; replicating the stance. And so it began.

His opponent left the ground.
Rotating one hundred and eighty degrees like
a spinning top to strike with a tobi ushiro
geri (back kick)

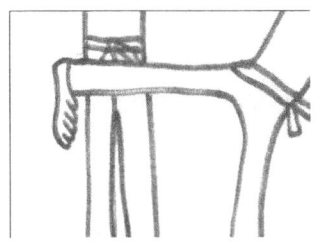

Sony dodged the kick; surprised at the imminent
momentum of the fight which continued with the enemies

Todi koke geri (spinning kick): pivoting a
turn of three hundred and sixty degrees with
the legs in complete straightness like a
helicopter.
Sony gave a flucky mae gedan barai block,
sending his arm in a vertical sweep
downwards, the blocking hand was held at
waist level:

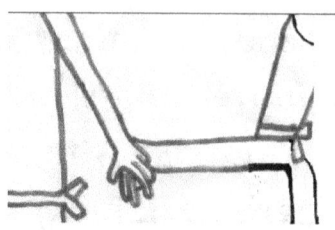

The kick struck above; hitting the arm at it to chest level (and if it wasn't for the strength of Sony's muscles the accident would not have been successful). But it snapped him into action

And his focus gave rise to an ascending age hiji ate elbow strike: knocking into the man's chin and leaving him exposed for the concluding

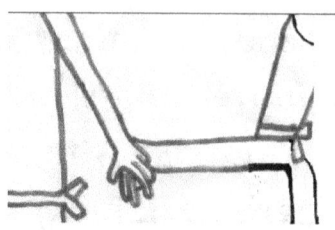

kagi tsuki swinging punch; forcing the man's stomach to hit the ground.

Knockdown. And now Sony was in the zone and the thirty second break allowed him to consciously enhance his fighting acuteness. The only thing that now existed were targets.

The fights that followed were explosive and every one was simplistic. Sony battled his way through various sequences of combat:

Blocking the sneaky kicks to his knee joint(kansetu geri) with a mae sune uke shin block in the tsurwashi dachi(crane stance)

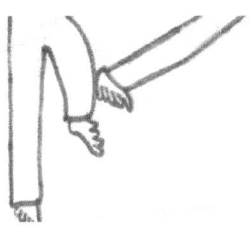

And then overthrowing the opponent with the heavy, butcher slicing potential of the shuto jodan uchi uchi (knife hand strike to the neck).

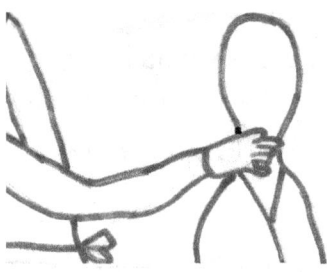

The battles were marked in his mind with blank seconds like a light bulb; flickering to moments of contact:

From when he distributed his energy from the centre to both sides of his body with the morote chudan uchi uke block to release the double handed grip of his opponent.

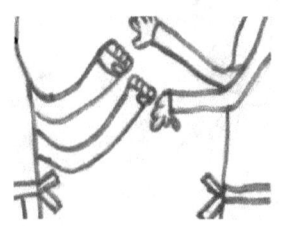

And the dive sideways whilst throwing the anchoring fist of the tettsui komekani to the side of the man's head; dropping him.

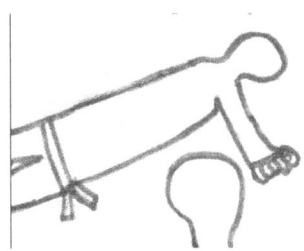

Or the eclipsing foot of the descending oroshi soto katato geri in the sky: smacking down on a man's attempt at a roundhouse kick; knocking him in the centre of his chest, shattering his upper body and so he falls.

The black light returns in Sony's mind only to return with

A tobi yoko geri jumping kick, the leg shooting out of the adversaries body like strips of lightning from clouds of thunder. But to Sony the advance was a traveling baseball and he just needed to bat in the right direction: the uchi mawashi keage hit perfectly (stretching a roundhouse kick diagonally from his body to the man's hip) curving him to the ground.

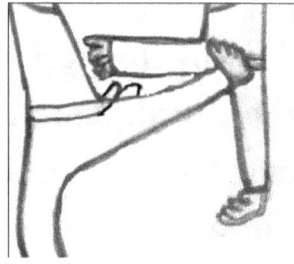

But it was now the thirtieth fight and Sony was exhausted. The stage was given to Ronald Walton: former European champion. Before that match began Sony already decided it was going to be a gigantic task.

The man swung down a lively elbow with a jumping oroshi hiji ate. One that came with a gravitational pull that Sony could even sense.

The impact would be intense. In those seconds he closed his eyes to except the blow that would explode on him; in that moment he left all of his fears behind him and simply decided to react (as the elbow descended it reminded him in milliseconds of the tea pouring at Mitcham) and a sudden aura entered his body like a flood of water.

And it rushed through his leg and swung as a koke geri (hooking kick): following the sweeping bends of a river's current; engulfing in a wide hook the area surrounding to catch on to the warrior, exploding with ki energy on the moment of impact: sending the man unconscious as he rocketed to the ground.

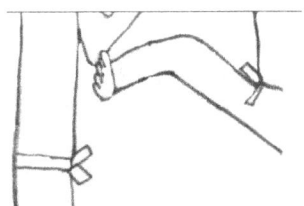

The moment was unexplainable and Sony felt freeness beyond comprehension. He looks to the flag in awe (noting the calligraphy form of kyokushinkai) "ah!! That's where it's from" he thought; envisioning the calligraphy of

Linda's cup in the park. He may have been in shock at the event but all he cared about is that he felt invincible (a second wind perhaps).

A calmness and relaxed sense of feeling permeated through the superseding matches (but with it also came a natural phenomenon of power and technical precision) unknown to Sony in his life's training.

The yoko geri (sidekick) is shot from an opponent as a steel shell of a shotgun: the leg loaded back into the chest to advance forward. So Sony's mae kaji uke front upper leg block uses the upward speed

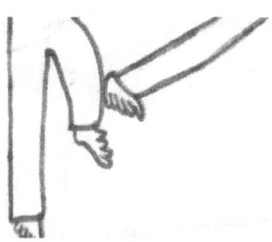

To spring the other leg in a turn to a back kick that smoothly bursts on his opponent.

And the series begins again. The audience looks on; shocked at the awesome demonstration of lighting fast, explosive technique. But to Sony the matts are now an ocean and each move is a slow drift which he sees clearly. The next enemies

Stretched punch in the zenkutsu dachi stance (the front knee bent deep whilst the back leg remains straightened) gathers brilliant sounds as it makes its journey. Only to find Sony's toho body part counter attack (an arch handed grip); the encased palm smacking against the man's throat to choke him on his own tongue until he drops.

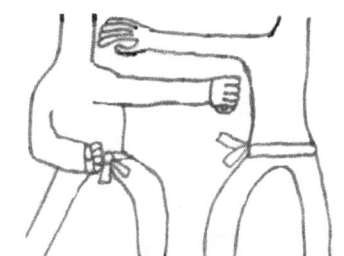

Sony loved every moment of it:

From the basic shift as the enemy goes for him and a tettsui yoko uchi bottom fist strike

to the side, turning a tornado like spin to face his back to his opponent whilst discarding a tree from the spin that is a thrown fist in the man's gut

And the tides draft in another fool's yohon nukite (four fingered spear hand strike) like a jagged sea shell. Erupted upon by a headbut in the statement of power; smashing the fingers.

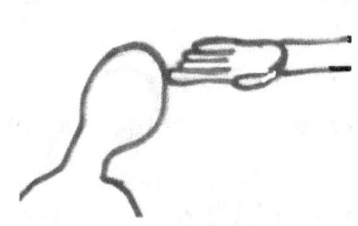

Then (after forty nine full contact kumites) the last fight is here. Sony is so close to completion and in this fight he could take no chances; not after this. Not here. Not now.

The tobi mae geri (jumping front kick) leaves the ground: the leg travels forward but Sony is already side by side with the enemy now And the uchi mawashi keage (inside roundhouse kick): sinks his foot in a terrible curve to the man's rib; levelling him in a bend. And the last move was definite

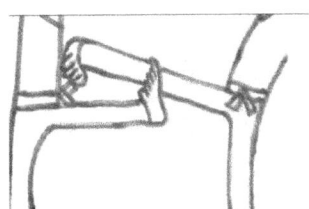

And a proclamation of his power: an oroshi sato kakto geri(downwards outside heel kick) sends a direct gravity dropping foot into the man's head, knocking him unconscious.

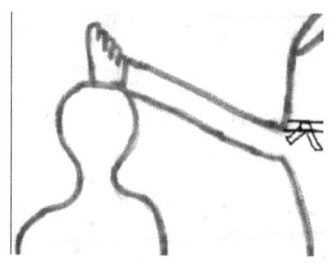

Sony is drenched in blood and bruises (he looks like he never won) but he bows to his opponent, he bows to the judges and (whilst the first aid team take the man away) the referee goes up to him and lifts his hand in the air. "Winner!!!" As he shouts the announcement the people send vibrations through the room with a chorus of exhausted screams, claps, whistles and shouts that reach him. It was electrifying and the arena's eyes were on him (he could feel it). But the serenity of the fighting euphoria had left him and he was left with the feeling of emptiness; (he couldn't understand it) the final fight had left an ache in his stomach that sickened him (the mere memory of it uneased him). He escaped the crowds in haste by telling admirers that he needed to rest. He retired to the car and smoked a cigarette; beginning to reflect on what just happened. He blew the grey smoke and (for the first time in his fighting career) he felt remorse.

CHAPTER 9: ROGER'S PRIDE

'Emphasis on the physical aspects of warriorship is futile, for the power of the body is always limited.'
- Ueshiba Morihei, The founder of Aikido

The time had reached three o' clock. The final break on the program had concluded and it was time for the black belt tournaments. The mats were littered with the rubble of bricks and wooden boards, foot dust and blood of the lower ranks. They were still clearing the mats with brooms and mops. The students were recreating the competition trials: new tiles of concrete were piled up and the mats were put back together. The judges convened to their seats and the referees stepped on the tournament floors.

As black belts began to prepare they were seated on front row seats (some of them stretching and others like Sony, Roger and William were tying rope around their feet). The referees began to call people's names and so the contestants took to the floor; the patterned mats were stationed with ten black belts who began sequences of combat. The other mat had a single row of students watching one of their peers swing his arm down into slates of concrete (shattering the first two but failing to penetrate the rest). However (amongst all of this excitement and activity) the trio's focus remained firmly on centre stage; they were in individual bubbles of focus (replicated by other serious fighters around the hall) watching the first combatants; aching to enter the tournament. Then Roger's moment finally came as the three were sitting with their girlfriends. As he left Kate she gave him a long, withering kiss (as though she was never going to see him again); giving an intentional pressure to an already stressful moment. He left her and walked onto the mat (prepping himself at the same time). He stood in front of his opponent; a somewhat feeble looking, skinny Scotsman with ginger hair (which only added insult to injury). However Roger didn't care much for this; he simply wanted the man out of the way so he could get to the next match. The referee began the bowing procedure and Roger's mind was slipping into the abyss.

He extends his left leg whilst bending his knee and pivots the back foot so that it was pointing in the sideways direction of his body. The clenched fists are raised across his chest and his face and now mind turn blank:

His arm swings like a sledge hammer as he circles to the man's ribs with a kagi tsuki (hooking punch) that just connects in the leaning effect of the zenkutsu dachi stance:

But the man turns forty five percent to line his body with Roger's, entering the shiko dachi (sumo stance): his legs parallel; separated with a big bend in the knees for balance whilst firming Roger's advances. He then simply uses a jun tsuki (average punch) from his shoulders to smack Roger in the face; sending thc man tumbling slightly backwards. He was not amused.

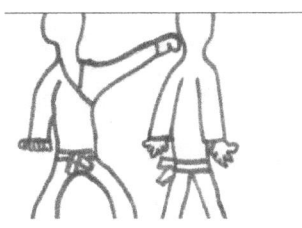

So Roger attempts to over whelm his foe with a flurry of uncoordinated grenades, but the man was unaffected. Instead his response was an equal measure of twisting blocks continuously turning the sides of his hand. Roger propelled a tobi hiza geri (sending an air defying knee strike) only to have the wind knocked out of him by a faster ushiro geri (back kick): smacking into his chest and landing his entire being on the mat.

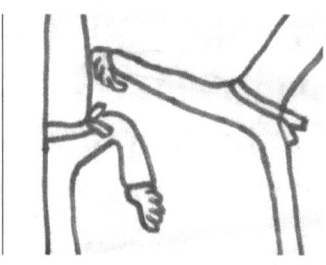

As his feet hit the floor he was no longer mindless and was squarely brought back to the awkward reality (the inevitable fear of a superior opponent). The enemies advance continues with

A tobi yoko geri (jumping side kick): propelling the flying ball of muscle a metre forward before the leg extends like the wings of a descending crane: entirely dedicated to the target. And Roger reacts with a Tobi hiza geri knee once again; simultaneously.

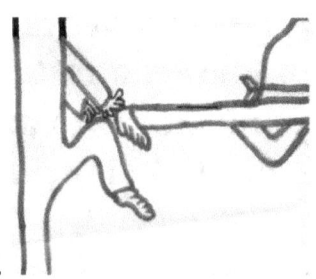

The combatant begins to smirk, he is amused by the challenge he receives and he

Bends both of his knees, keeping one leg slightly in front of the other; using his hips to create a ninety five percent shift of weight to his back leg in the nekoashi dachi (cat stance): his leg then circles in the air like the drawing of a perfect circle: the pen of his foot scratching down in momentum towards Roger's shoulder

But the fun is cut short when Roger executes a teisoku sato mawashi (inside roundhouse foot block): with a swinging leg that circles similarly to his adversaries

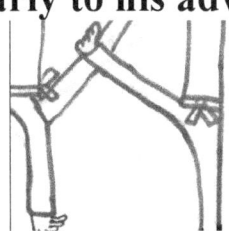

But the attacker was not finished.

He imposed a tobi kake geri (jumping spinning kick) on the spot: knocking Roger's cheeks into rotation and carrying his body with it (making his head spin like he would be defeated).

He looks into the crowds to seek the only audience who could shame him and there she was (her eyes unchanging as if void of all emotion). But the vision left him as his chin moved up as a result of a

Jodan uchi haisoku geri (vertically ascending kick).

It should have been a knockout but it wasn't. And as he fell back on his feet her words in the car at Coulsdon whispered from his mind: "NO MERCY". He lands

In the straightened leg stance of the sanchin dachi(hourglass): both feet turned inwardly extending his arms sharply with his knuckles turned at the enemy.

The anger that took him had returned. The enemy would be overcome; he was in the way and deserved no holding back:

The man advanced with an ago jodan geri (high front kick to the chin) to finish the job once and for all; but Roger smashes down on the leg with the hira kate (back part of his arm): attacking and defending simultaneously.

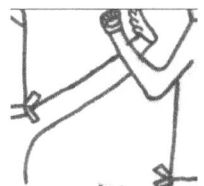

The feeling on the mat was now twisted and heavy. It became the savannah of a lion. But the opponent was desperate to not snatch defeat from the jaws of victory and

Descends his fist with all of his will into a tettsui oroshi ganmen uchi (bottom fist strike to the head): and it lands but Roger's eyes were unchanged.

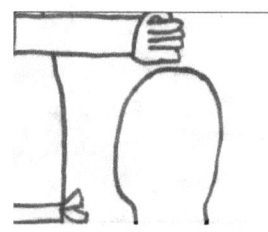

But the man is unconvinced and again he strikes; this time with an uppercut towards his stomach. It is now too late; Roger blocks and conquers the attack with his elbow using the hidji (part of the elbow covered in muscles); used many times to break wooden logs: killing the nerves of the adversary's fist.

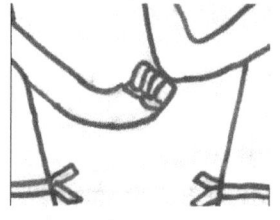

Roger then charges forward with his oi tsuki (lunge punch). There was no stance, no technique and only a ruthless resolve. Instead of a fist, the drained opponent received an uraken (knuckles of the middle and index fingers): focused at the centre of his head for the shocking power needed to make the opponent dizzied near to unconsciousness

And then to his forehead with a backfist strike (with the same body part). But Before he even has a chance to move to fall, he is knocked unconscious with a sword like oroshi hiji ate (falling elbow): bringing the man to inevitable loss of consciousness.

And if it's the last thing Roger does he will make sure this man does not continue the kumite; (he will fall) he is prey for the lion and a threat. So he takes to the air moving all of his muscles to finish it. He

Kicks the man twice with a tobi nidan geri(jumping double kick): smacking him in both

pecs finally allowing him to fall crippled and struggling in pain.

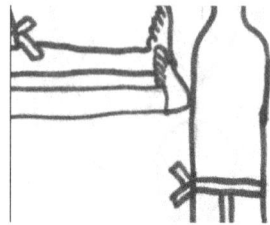

He reaches the ground proud and bows to the fallen. The referee calls the first aid team in to carry the man down to the changing rooms and Roger leaves the mat to sit with the others (completely without remorse). He has burned allot of energy and William smirks; passing him water as they clean the blood of off the mats (moping it until shiny like at the begging of the tournament). Roger reached a clap from the black belts who cared; the others in the hall would only cheer for the true champion.

CHAPTER 10: WILLIAM'S STRIKE

'The man who would be a warrior considers it his most basic intention to keep death always in mind, day and night, from the time he first picks up his chopsticks in celebrating his morning meal on New Year's Day to the evening of the last day of the year. When one constantly keeps death in mind, both loyalty and filial piety are realized, myriad evils and disasters are avoided, one is

without illness and mishap, and lives out a long life. In addition, even his character is improved. Such are the many benefits of this act.'
-Daidoji Yuzan, author of Budoshoshinshu

The referee came back to the Matts and circled his eyes around the front rows to gather the black belts attention once again. He was an average weighted short man with a shiny bald head; wearing a white polo shirt and straight black trousers with a whistle hanging from his thick neck. He blows the whistle and every eye is on him. "David Major verses William". The two men stood up and William looked down at Louise who mildly scowled at him (due to expectation) and then rubbed his hand softly. He walked onto the matt and met David Major. The two stood eye to eye (the hunger clearly voiding all sense of a previous friendship) and exchanged bows; entering the moroashi dachi stance (extending the left leg and arm at shoulder width level whilst extending the right arm at waist level) both with opened hands. To William the matt was a cold shock on his feet and he was trapped in a bubble (it was a vacuum where time and space seized to exist) and he was solely in the moment.

The same coldness was also surrounding the fallen Joey Santez (who was being nursed by the first aid tea). He had a gash at the top of his eye and a blood fountain that was called his nose whilst patterning his body were various swellings on his hands and feet, patches of purple running up his leg and small razor like cuts across his chest (in short the man was wrecked). His eyes were watering and every breath was a moan. The team rubbed cotton buds and place ice on his wounds; holding his neck to force feed him water. The tournament continues.

William charges forward with a jodan uchi haisoku geri(upwards axe kick) and found a soto yoko keage(side stretch kick) to match it

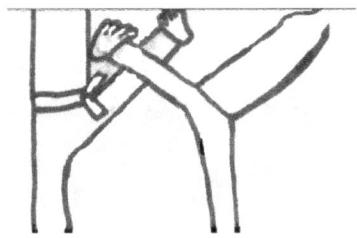

William diverts his attack in response with a clever teisoku soto mawashi uke(inside roundhouse foot block): circling his leg through the air like a tornado; halting the advance by smacking his face (which turns intensely) bringing his body with it

So he persists: swinging his leg like a holla hoop with an intense speed; spinning 360 degrees around his body ending with the tobi ushiro mawashi geri(backwards round house kick): into the man's back spinning him in another semi circle until

He hastily regains his ground and attempts a hasty backfist punch (uraken shomen uchi) which is cut dead with a gyaku tsuki (reverse punch): executed by pulling one arm back to spring the other arm forward; smacking into William's heart where his ego lied.

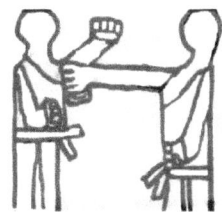

And his heart struck back with a shuto jodan uchi uchi(knife hand strike to neck): bolting his knife hand in a short descending sweep to the man's neck; giving him a slight stumble to the side.

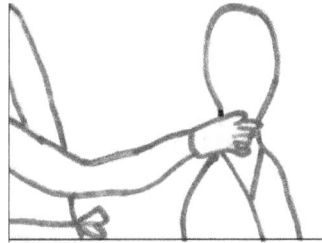

William attempts to seize the opportunity by thrusting a tate tsuki (vertical fist) with the extended hand format of the hiraken(open palm with closed knuckles): to send the shock power technique to the centre of the man's body.

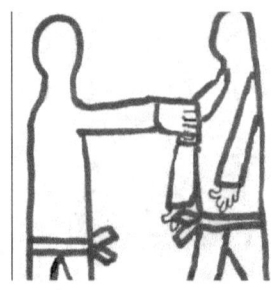

Then aims for a finale by running into a headbut with the rugged atman (part of the head): driving it with the same violence into the man's chest that left Roger's foe broken.

And Joey was still in the changing room and his breathing was slowing down (like a meditative process) but the first aid experts didn't feel that this was the case. And now they put the cold equipment onto the man's heart and listened to its rhythm; it was a fast African drum played relentlessly by a man in a trance. Through Joey's eyes he could see past the watering to a blurry vision of blue lockers and he could

feel the concrete flooring. His senses were intensified and exaggerated in his mental state.

But for William the fight was not over. The man finds his feet and pursues with a hiza ganmen geri(knee kick to face): bringing William's face into the man's knee joint and follows it up with an age tsuki (uppercut)

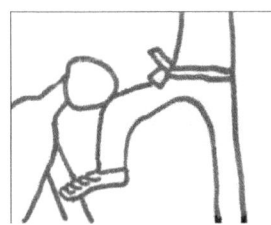

William was becoming tired; but he uses his brain and musters the strength to turn his back as a startling deceptive age kakato ushiro geri(rising heel backwards kick): flicking his leg up in a sharp move to the man's leg; taking him of balance.

To give William the time to turn and face his opponent; smacking him in the top of his head with a jumping roundhouse kick that bolted with a harsh wind behind it

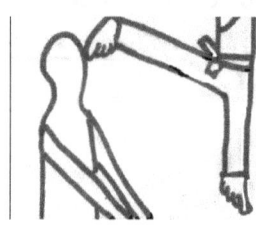

He refuses to stop the attack and goes in for a jodan uchi haisoku geri(knee kick to face): flicking his leg from his knee joint to the adversaries' chin. But the opponents osu(determination) is strong and he rises to the challenge with a osae uke (pressing down block): crossing his arms in an x and holding the attack in the space between them.

William was now panicking; the man wouldn't fall and he could lose everything (to be the best was everything). In this desperate moment the most sinister thoughts were formed into technique and (even worst still) he put his heart behind the moves

He moved into the security of the horse stance and executed a uraken mawashi uchi (circular punch): moving his swing in a semi-circle towards the side of the man's head but as the punch soared with the momentum of a rollacoaster

William changed his hand structure to the nakajubi ipon ken (extending the middle finger's knuckle and securing it by pressing down on it with the thumb): creating the precision and power of a speeding bullet. And it hit the man's temple. He twisted in an immense fall to the ground, floored with a mangled torso; his eyes white.

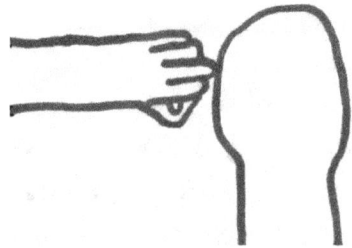

The crowd fell silent and gazes of five thousand shocked persons lingered. The referee checked the pulse of the man and gave a shocked look to William. He turns to the judges; giving the death signal and the gazes of the masters turn to cold discontent. But the moment was broken by a black belt who rushed towards the fallen warrior (bowing at his side with tears that spoke); telling them who he was: Ricky Major; the man's cousin. William was still entrapped by the bubble and he could hear nothing; his muscles and veins were still gasping in and out and his eyes were firmly fixed on David Major (but he felt nothing. He thought nothing). Then the hall began to change: there were people rushing around WIlliam and angry faces came towards him like a gas cloud (ready to take him with suffocation). Students swarmed towards him in hundreds and the muffled shouts began to break through. The final penetration came when his own class mates sprung to his defence and a violent fight erupted in the sports hall (but still William stood paralysed). He turned to his left and sure families running out of the arena hastily. Suddenly appearing hastily towards him were Kate, Louise and Linda; they grabbed him (shouting in his ears) but the young man dropped to his knees in a pit of confusion and disbelief. Chaos ensued his entire vision; the arena had been turned inside from out and the masters were ringing the authorities (whilst the sports centre's employees and managers cowered).

Meanwhile Sony was smoking a cigarette in the car. He had finally managed to take his mind of the concerns of the kumite (but he was still maintaining it with deep breathing). It was now raining and drops were sliding down the roof and windows. He looked to his left and sure a wave of blue quickly passing; so he turns on the wind wipers to see police (armed with batons) running towards the leisure centre as the sounds of the beeping sirens of the armoured cars behind him became prevalent. He runs after them and passes the crowded reception area (following the officers trail) and as they enter the sports hall he sees them disperse as the twenty strong force begins to battle down and separate crowds of violent fighters (hundreds scattered across the hall). The emotions in some were uncontrollable; they fought the officers and flying kicks alongside fists were drawn to a halt by the smacking of batons. Floods of back up came to keep the peace. Sony looked around the chaos; in the centre he sure his class mates circling William and the ladies clinging besides him (behind them he noticed a paramedic team picking a man up and putting him on a table). He begins to struggle through the riot when (at the same time) the team of first aiders run up to the paramedic and Sony notices the face of the man they're carrying: Joey Santez (now a corpse). He sees Roger amongst the defenders but now he himself is circled amongst fighters (and karate is swinging in all manner of directions). "What could have happened?" Is the thought carried alongside Sony's banging run. He finally reaches the heart of the disruption and finds himself in the position of a peace keeper; trying to hold of the enemy lines surrounding and (inevitable) police disruption. He couldn't help but feel as though he is an alternative reality; a day of beauty had descended into ugliness as the once ultimate UK karate celebration is now the scene of the worst martial art riot seen in the history of the British Isles. The last thing he remembers was a referee pointing at him (from the corner of his eye stuck to the corner) and then his face slams on the floor and his tongue tastes of blood; as the police officer straps the metal handcuffs on him (with his knee lodged on Sony's rib cage). He shouts rights in Sony's ear: "you are under arrest for the attempted murder of Ricky James. You do not have to say anything when questioned and anything you do say can and will be used as evidence mate!" It was all too much; he passed out and everything dissolves before him.

CHAPTER 12: THE RESOLUTION

"The fastest way to attain courage is to follow the chosen Way and be willing

to abandon life itself for the sake of justice."
-Mas Oyama, the founder of Kyokushinkai karate

Sony awoke in a bleak cell on a cold, single mattress. He lifted his torso up and looked around the darkened box; there were no windows, a small hole in the floor (that bared the slight comparison of a toilet) and then nothing. He felt the stings of various cuts and bruises (from the day that had just passed). Lingering, thick air was breathing into the wounds through the baggie tracksuit bottoms he was wearing; they were grey and he was also wearing a matching hoddie (a statement of prison environment). His expression was bewildered; (mimicking his mind set) he was spaced out and even when he attempted to recall the events that led to this situation he couldn't relate (he was completely detached); it was just like a movie playing in his head. In the middle of this film a metallic bang cut the transmission and Sony's eyes turned to the solid iron door in front of him. It opened slowly as a very built police officer (armed with a long black cosh and wearing the dark blue attire of the metropolitan police) came through the door. "Someone named Linda has covered your bail. Follow me" said the rough, discontented voice. Sony didn't think; he simply followed the man down the cell hallway and into the front office. A chubby, mature woman in a white skirt was sitting at the front desk and Sony noted the see thru, plastic bag next to her. Then his attention diverted to a pale faced woman (with really messy, uncombed hair) wearing a creased, plain white dress sitting on a chair. Linda looked at Sony and bolted from the chair; covering him with an embracing hug and rubbing her cheek against his. He looked at her eye to eye and they both stood in silence (the only sound that broke was the dripping of Cingular tears falling from her bagged eyes). The woman at the desk called out "Mr Sony; here's your clothes and possessions. You're bailed for the next two weeks and then you return before you stand trial. If you breach your bail we'll be forced to take active measures to pursue you." Sony returned an empty agreement, signed a form and followed Linda to the car.

She didn't turn to look at him once as they went into the car. Sony kept his attention to the window; (watching the passing streets and people) mustering the courage to ask the unavoidable: "what the fuck happened?" He mumbled loudly (vainly attempting to keep his chaotic emotions under control). Linda kept her eyeshot to the roads (speaking coldly). "You really don't remember? Well I know almost as much as you; what I do know is that you're going down for GBH and your friends have even bigger problems". Sony's heart started to beat faster. "I need to see Roger and William", "that's who we're going to see now. This is such a mess". Her voice was depressed and flat. Sony could tell he couldn't reconcile her (nor was he armed with the knowledge to do so); all he could do is wait and watch the journey. The car passed the bending roads of South Norwood and past the major, East Croydon train station, turning to pass the various tram stops and hills. The car sped up as it entered the suburban Shirley area and it was at that point Sony realised where they were heading: to the dojo. They pulled up outside the church hall and the doors were opened. Sony feared this entry but he had to know what took place. They left the car but Linda stood and looked at him. "You have to go in by yourself; I can't come. Call me when you're finished". She didn't even wait for Sony's reply; she simply got back into the car and left him standing there to take the last steps into the dojo. He walked in and sure the whole class. All thirty students gazed at him and (lowering their gazes to the ground) they circled around their master. William and Roger were standing next to the sensei (and still no one said anything). Sony walked up to join the crowd and they parted to give him space. He looked up to his master who nodded in recognition of his disciple; the nod was returned and the students brought their minds to the hand held radio in the master's hands. The voice of the news reporter echoed in the hall: "a very good afternoon to you. I'm John Wilks and you're listening to BBC radio four. Two men were killed yesterday and one man seriously injured at Crystal Palace sports centre during a full contact karate tournament (three men have been arrested in connection with the offences). The Kyokushinkai association and London development council have apologised to the parents of the deceased; the ministry of defence has announced that effective immediately, all styles and schools of kyokushinkai karate are banned in the United kingdom until further notice. In other news..." The mood in the hall changed and all were silent whilst the master turned the radio off. "Students, this is a sad day for our art. Because of the events that transpired yesterday all the schools are closing across the UK. But don't blame Sony, Roger or William; we all know it wasn't their intention for this to happen. If you remember nothing of what I have taught you, remember these words: the doors of Kyokushinkai schools may be closed but the spirit of Osu will always be open to our hearts (it guides us through life and they can never shut the door on that..)" As the sensei was giving his final speech Sony's mind drifted into the reflection of his thoughts in the car the day before (he finally understood why he felt what he felt) and he couldn't help it: he exploded inside. "Sensei! Don't make excuses for us; you tried to teach us the true spirit of karate. We were fools. You taught us discipline, self-control and humility (all the things we never believed in). We just wanted to fight but now I understand that it's much more than that: the spirit of osu is not defeating one man (or a hundred), it's perfecting yourself. It's pushing the boundaries of success for all human beings and (above everything) it's about your will to become the best. We maimed and killed three good men for our selfish desires. They all strived to be the best and we may be more proficient fighters but they are the true champions because even a man's character should be perfected (mind, body and spirit)". Sony dropped to his knees and bowed to the ground. "Even if you never wish to see me ever again sensei I understand and I accept it. But please forgive me". The students were all silent and the master speechless (there was a mixture of shock, despair and admiration). William and Roger also fell to their knees and bowed. The students simultaneously threw their fists in the air; shouting "Osu!"

The Kyokushinkai School was officially closed.

THE END